# DREAMWALKER:
# NATIVE GUIDE

# DREAMWALKER: NATIVE GUIDE

David C. Dillon

iUniverse, Inc.
Bloomington

# Dreamwalker: Native Guide

iUniverse books may be ordered through booksellers or by contacting:

iUniverse
1663 Liberty Drive
Bloomington, IN 47403
www.iuniverse.com
1-800-Authors (1-800-288-4677)

ISBN: 978-1-4759-4412-9 (sc)
ISBN: 978-1-4759-4413-6 (ebk)

Printed in the United States of America

iUniverse rev. date: 08/23/2012

# CONTENTS

# PREFACE

I wrote this book to share with others some of the experiences of my own dreams and my travels to South Dakota and meeting some of the wonderful Lakota people. I wanted to share a vision quest that changed my life while visiting that beautiful state. I hope you enjoy reading this book and I welcome any comments.

Remember, when dreams become a reality then reality is a dream.

David C. Dillon

# ACKNOWLEDGMENTS

This book is dedicated to my mom, my two daughters and my two granddaughters.

It is also dedicated to my very good friends on the Pine Ridge Reservation in South Dakota, John, Terri, Danishia, April, Joanna, and Grandma (Rest in Peace) whom without them this book would not have been possible.

This book is fiction but many of the chapters are based on true stories and experiences.

# INTRODUCTION

This is a story of how one man uses his dreams in everyday situations and how his dreams guide him and protect him. It is based on the abilities of a little known secret society of the Lakota people with the skill to dream about their future.

The secret dream society knew that people with this ability could not make what they wanted to happen by just dreaming it. The dreams were random acts during sleep but could be used, with practice, to see ahead and change what might be. They also realized this ability was passed down generation after generation through the blood line. One had to be born into it.

If this secret dream society was so secret how did Conley know about it? Was it because his grandmother was Lakota or was it because he dreamed it?

# CHAPTER 1

C onley is trapped between two webs and tangled in both of them. He sees that both webs have elegant patterns, the white one is made from a spider and the other one is made from light blue wax string with an eagle feather stuck to it. He feels one will harm him and the other will save him but both will have a major impact on his life.

Conley doesn't see any spiders but just seeing the web gives him that creepy crawly feeling he gets when thinking about them. He can feel one of the eight legged things walking on his head. He is unable to knock it off and he sure doesn't like that feeling. He shudders and then feels the spider web sticking to his hand and face.

He recognizes the old Native American woman he has seen many times before. She is holding a rose in one hand and she is motioning with her other hand for Conley to come over to her. He doesn't know this lady and wonders why he feels such a strong bond with this woman.

Next Conley sees a beautiful teenage girl looking in a mirror. She has blonde hair and a ponytail but the image in the mirror has brown hair and a ponytail. Conley watches as both girls walk through some snow to his back door. Conley was surprised to see these girls coming to visit him. Also, Conley doesn't understand seeing the snow this time of year.

Conley tries to move toward the girls but he is still trapped by the spider web. When he pulls on the web it sets off an alarm.

The alarm was going off. Conley woke and remembered the dream. He stretched his six foot lean frame then he got out of bed and got dressed. He looked outside and sure enough there was the snow. Because of his dream he knew he was going to get company.

Conley's dreams usually came true. They helped him by allowing him to see what was going to happen before it took place. This happened frequently to Conley. His dreams were random pieces of information he could use that helped him save his life sometimes and the lives of others. His only problem was figuring out the dreams and what they really meant. His dreams usually were more like puzzle pieces he had to fit together to make sense of them in order for them to be useful. For Conley that wasn't always easy.

Conley headed outside to clear the walk and steps of snow before anyone arrived. He was in good shape for someone almost forty years of age. He worked out a few times a week and only watched television a couple hours a week unless there was a Cincinnati Reds baseball game on or the Indianapolis Colts were playing. He was the type of guy that liked doing things instead of watching things being done.

The snow was deep and beautiful. He loved how it covered the land and gave everything a fresh new look. There were only a few tiny bird foot prints to disrupt the all-white blanket. Since nothing was ever perfect the little bird foot prints now completed how he felt about life, enchanting even when it's flawed.

Conley saw almost everything and everyone as being near perfect until it was proven otherwise. He looked at the footprints and thought they represented his dreams which kept him in check with reality. He knew he saw the world as basically a good place but deep inside he knew there were pockets of evil and his dreams brought him back to the way things really were.

Most people had dreams to escape reality but Conley used his dreams to connect with what was real. He knew without them he would be lost.

After finishing outside, Conley stomped the snow off his boots and closed the back door. Conley had been out less than an hour this morning sweeping the snow off the walk and steps to his tin can castle as he called his trailer. He didn't know why he felt he had to sweep off the walk and steps each time it snowed, even two or three times a day if it continued to snow. He hardly ever had company but today was going to be different. He always cleared the snow away; it just made him feel better. Besides he wouldn't want the neighborhood kids to slip and fall going up to his door to ask if they could shovel the snow off his walk.

Conley heard a car pulling into his driveway and he heard car doors slamming shut. He heard loud voices and couldn't understand why there was so much yelling. As he got up to go see what was going on outside there was a knock at the back door.

The back door opened before Conley could get there. One girl walked inside and another girl backed into the room still yelling back to the car.

"Mom, drop it, okay? Man, I can't wait until next year when I get my own driver's license," Morgan yelled. She took off her coat and tried to throw it on top of the dryer and when it fell to the floor she clinched her fist and said, "Gawd, stupid stepdad."

Morgan was thin and full of energy. Conley knew she fought hard to get her way and didn't back down from any challenge. She just had to fight the good fight even if it was over something that didn't matter.

Meredith walked over to Conley and gave him a hug and a kiss. "Hi, Daddy."

Meredith was about the same height as Morgan but not quite as thin. She had a freckle above the corner of her mouth on the left side which was the fastest way to tell her apart from her twin sister.

Morgan slammed the door shut and said, "Hi, Dad. Mom said to remind you that you turn forty at the end of this summer." She cracked a small grin.

Conley wasn't sure if the comment actually came from the girls' mom or if it was from Morgan who always liked to keep things interesting.

Conley replied, "Tell her thanks and that I love her too."

Meredith passed out some sausage and egg biscuits to everyone for breakfast.

Conley saw that Morgan had lightened her hair and had grown just a little taller than Meredith, or maybe it was from the difference in her wearing boots. He was pleased that they both were wearing the matching charcoal colored leather coats with the white rabbit fur collar he had given them for Christmas.

"What brings my sweethearts all the way from Kentucky to see me today?" Conley asked.

"Dad, it's not that far to Indiana from where we live, you know. We had a snow day today and Mom had to take a couple orders of her birdhouses over to some stores in Metamora and we came along to surprise you. We can only stay until she's done," Meredith said.

"Well, it's a nice surprise," Conley answered.

"No it isn't. You knew we were coming. You always do. You even cleaned the walk off before we got here. Stupid dreams," Morgan said.

"Oh, Dad, that reminds me. We need your help with something. Both of us are having dreams like you have. They freak Morgan out and they kinda scare me," Meredith said.

"You're the only one I've ever heard of that does this. It's freaky to watch something happen when you know how it's going to end. It's very frustrating and I don't know how to act or what to do when it happens. I hate them," Morgan said. "Make them stop."

"Most of the time we dream different things but sometimes we have the same dreams. I don't understand what's going on. What am I supposed to do?" Meredith asked.

Conley looked at both of his girls. His head dropped and he stared at the floor for several minutes. He didn't have an answer.

Finally Conley looked up and saw both girls searching his face for some sort of wisdom that would fix the problem.

"I don't understand the dreams either. In grade school I can remember when the dreams were so bad I knew everything that was going to happen. The teacher would turn his back to the class and write something on the blackboard and before he could turn back around so the class could see what he wrote I already had it written on my paper. When the teacher would ask the class a question I would turn and look at a certain girl raising her hand and the teacher would then call on that girl. I even knew what she was going to say. This sorta thing happened all the time with me.

"It got so bad at one point in my life that I couldn't tell if I was dreaming or if things were really happening around me. I was in a daze and it was hard for me to even function. At that young age I had no one who could guide me with my dreams. I thought everyone did this. I was shocked when, in junior high school, I learned that no one did this and people were actually afraid of me and made fun of me for my ability," Conley said.

"Well? How does that help us? Dad, this is serious. This crap really bothers me," Morgan said.

"Well, for one thing, you're not alone dreaming like I was. Each of you knows two other people that do this and together we will figure out what to do," Conley replied.

"Do you think Grandma does this? Maybe she can help," Meredith asked.

Conley learned only last year that his mother had dreams like his. She never spoke of them. He was surprised when it slipped out that she had the dreams. Since then, she has never brought it back up and hasn't talk about dreams since.

"My mom doesn't like to talk about the dreams. I don't think she understands them either. I do know her mom, my grandmother, has the dreams. I will make you both a promise right now. Whatever it takes, I will find the answers one way or another," Conley said.

The one time Conley's mom did talk about dreams, Conley learned his grandmother had the dreams and even saw and talked to people that had passed away in her dreams. It had been many years since Conley saw his grandmother and they had never talked about dreams.

She was a full blooded Native American. His mom was too, but once Conley's mom married a white man she wasn't considered Indian any longer by the tribe and had to leave the tribe and the reservation. She could have stayed but she wouldn't have been accepted any longer.

So, she left with her husband for a life where Conley's dad could find work. Except for family, no one ever knew his mom was Native American and the only hint being her jet black hair.

Conley felt it was due to his mom's religion why she never liked talking about the dreams. The church she went to didn't believe in any supernatural powers for humans, therefore, anyone that could do any of these type things were receiving gifts from the devil. That was the main reason Conley didn't go to church any more. He knew he dreamed and he wasn't a bad person because this gift had helped him and many others in the past. That was a good thing, not something evil. To him, they were just simply dreams that happened, not some kind of supernatural powers.

Conley had grown up with his dreams. He learned to accept them and how to use them to help him and others and keep them from harm's way most of the time. He had learned on his own what was going on and it was a very long and painful process. He didn't understand what it was all about or why they happened and now he needed to know to save his girls from experiencing all of the trouble he had to endure.

Most of the time he liked having these dreams, especially after he realized what was going on. At first, when he was very young, they confused him but now they were just a part of his life. He didn't mind them now that he knew what was happening and he knew more about how to use them. He still needed answers if he was to help his daughters.

"Dad how will you do that? How will you find great-grandma to get any answers? No one has heard from great-grandma for years and years now. No one even knows where she lives back on the reservation, do they?" Meredith asked.

"I made you both a promise so leave that up to me. I don't want you girls to go through what all I had to go through with these dreams," Conley replied.

"What are you going to do? Go out west with some blood hounds and track great-grandma down back in the mountains?" Morgan asked with a tone that implied she thought her idea was ridiculous.

"If I have to," Conley said without hesitation.

A car horn blew in the driveway. "That's Mom," both girls said and they jumped up and grabbed their coats. They gave Conley a kiss good-bye as they bolted out the door.

After his daughters left Conley was flooded with memories from his childhood. He knew that being part Indian explained why he had always played the Indian when he was young and playing cowboys and Indians as a little kid. He made sure the Indians won whatever it took until most of the other kids would no longer play with him because he didn't play right. Everyone knew the Indians didn't win.

When Conley got captured and had to throw down his guns he always had another gun in his waist band in the back of his blue jeans or a derringer in his shoe. Later when the other kids caught on to this and started searching him he would find, beforehand, where they were going to put him in jail and throw a gun near the jail in the weeds and would be able to reach it once he was confined there.

He could sneak up behind someone usually without ever being seen by crawling on his belly through the weeds and stay in that position for a very long time until some of the cowboys were close enough for him to jump them.

He could plan a battle better than all the rest. Conley would have what few braves were on his side start shooting and then sneak in behind the cowboys and take their fort.

Conley smiled at the thoughts of his childhood. He stopped smiling when he thought about his daughters' childhoods. He had missed so much of them growing up. Conley was there for them but on a limited basis. The girls' mother had left him and moved from southeastern Indiana to northern Kentucky when they were very young.

Conley thought he had to make the Indians win one more time. Conley's daughters now needed his help and he wasn't about to let them down.

# CHAPTER 2

Conley watched out the window and waved as his daughters left. He looked around at the white blanket covering the earth giving it one last nap before it burst forth with the energy of spring. The late snow, and hopefully the last snow of the season, came in on April first and as usual, snow this late in the season was very wet and heavy. What an April fool's joke nature had played on everyone this year with six inches of snow creating the fresh blanket of cloud dandruff, as Conley sometimes liked to call it.

The weight of the white snow had broken out the top seven or eight feet of the Christmas tree shaped blue spruce in the back of his property line up next the woods. Conley knew the tree would have to come down later this year once the weather was nice. Evergreen trees just don't make a comeback like some other trees can. It would live but it would never regain its top again and would always look broken.

Conley put a pot of water on the stove to heat for his morning coffee. He added two scoops of coffee grounds to the pot and turned the stove up so it would come to a boil. After it started boiling he would then let it simmer for a short time. He had to be careful pouring the coffee and pour it slowly or else he would fill his cup with a bunch of grounds and he would end up chewing the last few sips.

Conley thought of the dream of the old woman that was motioning with her arm for him to come to her. He had dreamed of the old woman many times in the last month and it was always the same; she was motioning with her arm for him to come to her.

Conley was in need of answers. He had to find out about his dreams in order to help his daughters. He thought this old Native American woman was a sure clue and he needed to know who she was. Was this woman his grandmother?

Conley would talk to his mom and ask what his grandmother looked like and try to get enough information to see if this old woman in his dream may be some distant relation. His mom didn't like talking about dreams so he would have to just ask out of curiosity.

As he grew up he had tried to learn how to use his dreams and learn more about what they meant. First he studied about the meanings of dream symbols but that didn't really have too much to do with how he dreamed. He studied about meditation and that didn't really help much either. So he just started writing down what he dreamed and started looking for clues of what they meant in his real life, his awake life.

Sometimes he would remember what was going to happen from his dreams. He learned things in his real or awake world would trigger a dream memory and then he would know a plan of action to consider, thus, getting a different outcome of what he knew was around the corner. His dreams gave him an advance warning of what was to be, unless he changed the events. He learned to use this to do good.

On the up side of him having these dreams, when he was a kid he would know to duck without even knowing someone just threw a snowball at him and the snowball would miss. He had great awareness of things around him because he was always looking for a clue that would awake a memory from a dream he just had. He naturally did this from training himself to be aware of everything around him over the years. It felt as if he had a bubble of protection around him that kept him safe.

Not all of his dreams were bad or about dangerous circumstances. Some of his dreams were just average dreams like anyone else would have. Some of the dreams were delightful and could be used for enjoyment of things happening around him. Other dreams were very simple like finding something he had misplaced and many of the dreams just made his life better.

There were times he would dream the same thing over and over. Some of these dreams he wouldn't always remember at first but when he did he paid greater attention because usually they had greater meaning about something that was going to happen. Then, all he had to do was look for the clues and be ready.

Conley walked over and glanced at the brochures he left out on the top of his desk. He loved to travel. He was planning to go on another trip as soon as all this cold weather was over. He had been several times on trips through the south, southwest and eastern seaboard. He was just considering where to go this year that he would enjoy. He was thinking about going north or west this time since those were the two directions he never traveled. And with spring not far off, it was time to start planning a direction to head off to visit, a place where he could camp and fish.

He had two friends that went up into Canada every year to fish. An airplane flew them back to a desolate area with a large lake and left them where they camped for a week. They always brought back coolers full of large walleyes and muskies. This was definitely on his "to do" list and was a possibility for this year's trip.

Conley grew up with a love for fishing. His father's parents owned a fishing lake when Conley was a young boy. There was an old wood frame building with a store and bait shop in the front and living quarters in the back. They were the first in the area to offer instant hot food and this was a long time before microwaves. They used a toaster oven to heat meals for the fishermen. Conley helped run the store and worked around the lake.

During this time Conley had dreams of a witch that threw dynamite and blew up the store. He didn't understand why he dreamed the same dream so many times. He just thought it was a bad dream until one night the building caught on fire.

Because he was aware and always looking for clues from his dreams, he was the first to smell smoke. Everyone was in the back playing cards when a pot on the stove caught on fire. Conley's uncle had been cooking some bear meat and had let the water boil completely out. The pot burst into flames and the fire shot up the wall. The old wall paper then ignited and in minutes the whole place was ablaze.

Because Conley knew what was happening and warned them, everyone got out the back door in time. The dream wasn't exactly like what happened but it had the same results. This taught Conley that his dreams weren't always true to life but showed him how the dreams worked and how he could use them.

Besides fishing, he also loved history and there was so much history out west. Growing up he watched all the cowboy shows and movies. He had a great interest in the days of the outlaws. Those few years of infamous bad guys only lasted about twenty years and Conley had a great understanding of that era of our country's history. He not only watched the shows and movies but he researched the true accounts and the how and why of the people that did these evil deeds.

He watched a lot of travel shows on television but most of those were too far away, over in Europe or Asia and he didn't have that kind of money. He hoped that someday he could go to other counties but knew inside he probably wouldn't get the chance.

Conley lived alone and was experiencing cabin fever from being inside so much during the past winter. He already had his fishing and camping gear out of the closet and cleaned and ready to go. He liked being around other people but usually took his vacations by himself.

When he was with others he felt he had to entertain them and cater to their needs and concerns which was less enjoyable than taking a trip by his lonesome. Vacationing alone, Conley could go where he wanted and stay as long as he wanted and do the things he liked. He never had to be at a certain place at a certain time and that made his trips much more enjoyable. Usually his friends had to work and since he only worked when he wanted or needed to he could get away any time he wished and stay as long as he liked. He made friends easily wherever he went so he always had new and interesting people to fill in his time. He was at home wherever he ended up.

Now he only wanted to find this Indian woman he thought must be his grandmother. Maybe he could make a trip out west and search for this women in his dreams and turn it into a vacation. This next trip could be something that would change his life.

Conley heard the mail truck and he looked as the mail carrier put a letter into his mailbox. Conley wondered if all the mail trucks came from England since they had the driver on the right side of the truck.

Conley trotted out and retrieved his letter and trotted back inside to open it. The hand writing on the envelope was large and hard to read. It looked as if someone had a hard time writing his address. He noticed there was no return address.

He opened the letter and read:

Conley,

I need to see you one more time before I go. I will come and visit you soon.

Grandma

# CHAPTER 3

An elderly woman is walking down a path leading a black and white pony with a white blaze or star on its forehead. She stops on a rise and is looking for something or someone. Her hair is gray and she has two braids one down each side of her face. She is wearing a long, light green, faded dress that comes down to her ankles and she has on what looks like only one old leather moccasin with sheep's wool around the top. Her face is weather worn and full of deep age wrinkles. She is average height but is slightly overweight.

The sun is setting behind her as she looks out over the trench of land below her. There are others on the path behind her but they are without form in the murkiness. She waits.

Conley spots her. He doesn't know where he is or what time it is. He just seems to be lingering there observing the old woman. She straightens up and holds out her hand in his direction. Then she makes a motion with her arm suggesting for him to come to her. She does this several times.

Conley asks himself, "Who is this woman? What does she want?" As soon as this thought comes into his mind the old woman smiles and nods her head. She grabs the pony's mane and pats her pony on the neck. She leads the pony back down the path, back toward the setting sun. She is gone.

Today Conley had to get busy. Today he had something important to take care of. His lot rent for his tin can castle was due and he also had to order another tank of propane for his heat.

He had hoped what he had left in the tank would last until warm weather got here but it didn't and he would need one more drop to carry him through the rest of spring. That meant he had to go to work today.

Conley worked at a river boat casino about an hour away from where he lived. He didn't work for the boat, he was a card player and gambled to earn what he needed to pay his bills and carry him through with his groceries and other expenses like his water and electricity. He liked his job because he set his own hours and didn't even have to go in but a few times a week, if that.

He arrived at the boat in midafternoon and walked down the gangplank onto the deck of the gambling boat which was docked on the Indiana side of the Ohio River. He went down the stairs heading for the lower deck where the card tables were located.

He was looking forward to seeing his friend Emily who was one of the dealers. He had met Emily a few years ago through one of his dreams and enjoyed hanging out with her ever since.

As he reached for the door handle to open the door leading to the main card room, the heavy metal fire door swung open very hard and fast. The door handle hit his thumb so hard he thought it was broken.

Two men came through laughing and were being very loud and obnoxious. The first man was wearing a business suit while the man behind him wore dress pants and shirt and had on a plaid jacket that didn't match anything Conley had even seen in the past twenty years.

Conley stepped out of their way toward the wall in the stair well holding his thumb and taking deep breaths to ease his pain. Conley was mild natured but that didn't mean he was a wimp.

When the men passed Conley heading for the stairs, one pushed the other into Conley and spilled his drink all over Conley's new pull over sweater and his tan suede jacket. They stopped. The one that spilled his drink pushed Conley and said, "Get out of my way, dork." The other man laughed.

"Excuse me?" Conley articulated.

"Damn right excuse you!" the rude man returned.

Conley tried to always treat others as if they were gentlemen. Not because they were necessarily but because he was. Conley was hoping his philosophy would work again today. "I didn't mean any harm but it was you that ran into me spilling your drink on my coat. You gentlemen owe me an apology and we will let it go at that," Conley announced knowing his coat was probably ruined.

The man laughed and said, "You spilled my drink and I think you better buy me another one before I knock your head off and spit down your neck."

"That isn't going to happen," Conley replied.

"Maybe I will make it happen, smart guy," was the drunk's answer.

"Yeah, let's show this guy some manners," the man standing to the rear said.

The man took a step toward Conley and grabbed his collar pushing him back against the wall. Conley took his right hand, his thumb still throbbing, across and over the top of the man's arm racking it loose and came back with the same arm and hit the man in the face using his elbow. The man's head snapped back and he stumbled several steps back and if it wasn't for the other man holding him up he would have fallen to the floor.

The man then threw his glass at Conley. Conley held up both arms in front of his face and ducked as the glass missed him and broke on the wall beside Conley.

Next the man came at Conley and threw a punch at his face. Conley blocked the punch and countered with a punch of his own, hitting the man in his solar plexus. The man leaned forward as a rush of air came from his lungs. Conley instinctively landed an upper cut punch to the man's chin knocking him back.

The man spit on Conley so Conley took a step past the man with one foot while the rest of his body was still facing the guy. This stance was called zenkutsu or front stance and was a powerful defense and counter move used in hand to hand combat. Conley then used a straight arm punch with his whole body driving his fist forward into the guy's nose. Conley saw the guy's eyes roll back into his head as the nose broke and started bleeding upon impact and he fell, this time to the floor and didn't move.

The second man attacked and grabbed Conley around the head and was trying to get him into a headlock with his right arm. While doing this, he landed a couple punches with his left fist hitting Conley in the chest.

Conley, struggling, lifted his right foot and with the heal of his dress shoe stomped down on top of the man's left foot hard enough to break more than a few of the bones along the top part of his arch.

The man wrenched in pain and lost the hold around Conley's head and neck. He almost lost his balance and had to hop to keep from falling down. Conley then opened his hand and slapped the man in the face as hard as he could to stun him. The man looked very surprised as Conley's open hand hit and went across his face and Conley came back using the outside edge of his hand to deliver a blow to the man's right temple.

The man seemed half out of it as Conley then snap kicked the man in the groin. The man doubled over, leaning forward and Conley using the same upper cut to his chin as he used on the guy's friend, knocked the man back. He stumbled backwards hitting the far wall of the stair well and fell forward to the floor on top of his friend.

Conley wasn't nervous during the fight but now that it was over he was shaking. The two men had picked the wrong guy to try and bully. Conley was a Vietnam veteran and he had taught self-defense as a teen in a local karate school even before he went into the military. He had fought in many karate tournaments as a teen but third place was the best he ever finished. He didn't consider himself a fighter. He had only learned how to fight to protect himself, to just be equal with everyone else.

As a youth he was very small and timid growing up. He was a late bloomer and didn't get his full height until he was in his early to mid-twenties so he was used to being bullied.

Conley went to open the door and had to use his foot to move one of the men's arms out of the way in order to get the door open. He stuck his head into the main card room and hollered for security. In a few minutes a security guard came to the door and asked, "What seems to be the problem here?"

The security guard was a thick, big boned hairy man with large hands. He was dressed in a police type uniform but looked more like a rent-a-cop instead of a policeman.

Conley opened the door all the way and the guard saw the two men on the floor. "Wow! What happened here?" he asked.

"These two came into the stair well and spilled a drink on me then attacked me. I defended myself and this is what is left," Conley told the guard.

The guard took his radio off his belt and said, "We need medical assistance in the stairs on the card room level and a tow truck."

"Tow truck?" Conley asked.

"Yep, that is what we call a paddy wagon so the other patrons don't get excited. We'll take these guys to the hospital to get them checked then haul them off to jail if your story turns out to be right. We'll review the security camera we have that shows this stairs and if what you say is true, and I have no doubt that it is, then these guys go to the clinger."

"Clinger?" Conley asked.

"Yep, you know, to the pokey. We provide a safe place here and don't take any type of trouble lightly. Looks like you could use some ice for that thumb of yours, too," the guard told Conley as he motioned for the barkeeper around the corner to get a bag of ice.

"Yes, I do need ice, thanks, and a stiff rum drink without ice," Conley returned.

Conley headed for the bar and sat with his rum and watched as two security guards took the two men, now in handcuffs, to the elevator. The barkeeper handed Conley the bag of ice. He was holding the bag of ice on his thumb wondering if he could concentrate enough to even play cards. He decided to just go home and come back tomorrow when Emily walked up and sat beside him.

Emily had on the black pants and white shirt which all the dealers had to wear. She had her hair pulled back into a pony tail and had a pink ribbon holding it in place. The pink ribbon was tied in a bow and the ends of the ribbons ran down to the bottom of her hair line.

"Heard what happened. You okay?" she asked.

"I think so unless my thumb is broken by those two butt wipes. Sorry, I should have said jerks. I think they did ruin my jacket though. Are you on break?" Conley took a napkin and blotted the stained area.

"No, on lunch. Want to go to the dining room and eat? I get a discount." Emily inspected the swelling on Conley's hand.

"That sounds good. It'll give me time to calm down. It doesn't look like I'll be able to play cards today anyway," Conley rose from his seat.

"Here, grab your drink and bring it with you." They both headed for the elevator to go up to the dining room.

The restaurant had a posh feel to it. The furniture was some of the finest money could buy. The tables were made of heavy wood and were far apart from each other. There were little half wall dividers with plants such as ferns or vines growing from the top of these half walls. The half walls gave beauty and privacy and also served to deaden any other sounds from other people.

They found a table and after they ordered Emily had to know all about what happened. As Conley told of the episode he could tell Emily got angry at the guys.

Emily said, "Those two guys were playing at the table next to where I was dealing. They were acting out almost too much for the other dealer to handle them. They had been asked to leave so I am glad you showed them the door the hard way. They deserved what they got."

"I'm not sure but I think it was them that showed me the door," Conley grinned and showed his thumb wrapped in ice to complete his pun.

Emily commented, "It's a shame you came all this way and now you won't get to play."

"No, I'm glad I came. I wouldn't have missed our lunch for the world," Conley smiled. "So everything worked out better than I could have wished for."

After they finished eating they took a walk over to the main floor exit and walked outside onto the deck of the boat. Not many people came out here to just look at the river, most were only interested in playing cards or gambling and wouldn't have cared where they were. This was one of the things Conley liked about Emily. She seemed to be able to observe everything around her and paid attention not only to what was going on but to the people she was with. Conley like that she listened to him and actually heard what he was saying when he talked.

Conley took his jacket off and put it around Emily's shoulders to keep the chill in the air from bothering her too much. He could smell a strawberry scent in her soft and shiny hair.

They saw a few small boats go by and a loaded coal barge lumbered by being pushed by a slow moving tug boat. Overhead loud squawking and honking noises drifted their way. A flock of Canadian geese flew by in their classic V-shaped formation.

It was peaceful outside and Conley could tell Emily enjoyed the fresh air. He felt she enjoyed just being with him. He sensed she enjoyed the stories and experiences he shared more than most people did.

He knew she was about the only one that could get him to open up and talk about all the things that had happened in his life. Conley didn't open up about himself very often and when he did it was usually with Emily. She was one of the few people Conley could trust, and for Conley, having one quality friend was worth more than having a dozen regular friends.

"I remember when we first met. I was your dream girl," Emily said to break the silence.

Conley laughed. "You still are my dream girl."

"You bought me coffee and we talked until I missed my bus. After that you were gone. Later that night on the news I heard where a woman on that very bus got shot and killed. It took me over a month to find you again to thank you. That's when you told me about your dreams and why you made me miss that bus.

"In the several years now that I have gotten to know you I know that when you are quiet you have something going on inside that head of yours. Right now though, I have to get back to work so will you call me later?" Emily asked.

"Yes, maybe you can help," Conley said. They turned and walked back inside, hugged and parted. He knew if he didn't confide in Emily she would stay on his case until she got his problem to surface.

# CHAPTER 4

The old Indian woman with long white braids rides her pony up a winding trail. Two Indian men join her. They are wearing rawhide pants, no shirts, and moccasins on their feet. Each has a band around his head. One band is made from braided porcupine quills and the other is a leather strap with a feather hanging down in the back. Both men have a small scar on both sides of their chests.

None have saddles but only use red blankets with some sort of eight pointed red star on each corner.

They ride their ponies across a stream and follow a winding trail through a small canyon. The old Indian woman leads the way with the two younger men not far behind her.

When they are all together they stop and look down at the ground. The younger of the two men gets off his pony and walks over to where they are looking. He picks up a rock and throws it back toward the narrow trail they had just followed through the pass. He then picks something else up. He shows the bone handle hunting knife with its ten inch blade to the others and walks on ahead carrying the knife until he comes to a tree that is growing almost sideway; he looks up and stops. He looks at the old woman. She gets off her pony and walks all the way around the leaning tree. She takes the knife.

She looks around then points to a flat rock about the size of a large skillet. The other Indian still on horseback dismounts and both men walk over and pick the rock up and move it very close to the tree trunk. The old woman puts the knife down next to the tree. The two *men then put the rock on top of the knife in such a manner that the knife can no longer be seen.*

*The three seem to be in agreement and get back onto their ponies. The old woman rides ahead a little ways until she sees a rather large buffalo on the path ahead and then she stops and looks back. She gives a motion with her arm that gesture for the others to join her. She does this several times but the others are gone.*

Conley was sealing the last of the bill envelopes for the month and he felt as good as he did on clean sheet day. He had enough money to cover all his monthly bills and some left over. His thumb had healed from last week and he had a very pleasant time winning the night before at the casino but still felt there was something left undone.

He had the strangest impulse, that nagging feeling, to go to his computer and check out something about his dreams. They had been bothering him and it was time for him to see why.

He went in and sat at his desk and at his computer he typed in Native American into the search engine. Within half a second he had over two hundred thousand pages to choose from.

Conley tried to organize his search instead of just clicking links and ending up with him reading about a canoe trip down some rapids somewhere which is what usually happened when he searched on the Internet. It was way too easy to get side tracked.

He started off by looking at all the reservations listed in the United States. He saw that his home state of Indiana didn't have any reservations. There were several Native American nations listed in the New England area: Cherokee listed in South Carolina, Seminole in Florida, and so on. He found that most of the reservations were out west. He read that one of the larger reservations was also one of the poorest. This one was in South Dakota and called the Pine Ridge Reservation.

He found the largest reservation in size is also the largest reservation in population called the Navajo Indian Reservation in Arizona and New Mexico. It looked as if Oklahoma had the most Indian reservations due to the Trail of Tears which was a forced removal of Indians east of the Mississippi River to Oklahoma. This was done by way of the Indian Removal Act of 1830 and caused thousands and thousands of Indians to die while making this journey.

Conley then checked out pages dealing with Native American chiefs. He read of Chief Blue Jacket who was a white man and a chief under Chief Tecumseh of the Shawnee tribe. They lived around Indiana in the late seventeen hundreds.

Next he read about Cochise and Geronimo of the Apache tribe and then of American Horse, Sitting Bull, Crazy Horse and Red Cloud of the Sioux or Lakota tribe. Conley found it interesting that Canada gave Chief Sitting Bull and his followers asylum from the United States at the end of the Indian wars against the Sioux and allowed Sitting Bull and his followers to live in Canada as free men.

A smirk came to Conley's face as he thought about the same thing happening for men in the United States as several moved to Canada to escape the draft during the Vietnam War.

Conley researched some of the great Indian battles and found most of them were mere massacres by the white man. His heart sank as he read of the Wounded Knee massacre and the Sand Creek massacre where seven hundred soldiers rode into a village and killed over one hundred and fifty peaceful Cheyenne and Arapaho Indians with two thirds of them being women and children.

Conley was interrupted by a knock on his door. He peered out as he passed by the window facing the driveway to see who was there. What he saw made him stop in his tracks for a second. There was a black limousine in his driveway with government tags.

At the door was an older, well dressed lady wearing a stylish coat with a fur lining around the collar and a tall man in a dark blue suit. The man said, "Hello, my name is Special Agent Henry from the CIA and this is Miss Violet. May we come in?" He held out a billfold with some sort of badge for Conley to inspect.

"Sure, please come on in," Conley said.

Miss Violet looked almost like the old Indian woman in Conley's dream. She was smaller in stature and thinner. She stood straight with her head held high and Conley could tell she was a proud woman. Her brown eyes were clear and her face was beaming with a light from within her. Her gray hair was fixed with two braids, one coming down each side of her face.

They walked inside and Miss Violet looked around and then went over and sat on the couch where she saw an Indian drum on the coffee table. She reached over and tapped the drum a few times with her fingers.

Conley said, "That's a Native American Shaman hoop drum. I made it myself."

"I know what it is. Did you follow the instructions and let one side face the morning sun and then the other side face the afternoon sun as it dried? Oh, that's right, you didn't have a set of instructions with it did you?" Miss Violet asked.

"I didn't have instructions but yes, that's how I made it. How did you know?" Conley asked.

"How did you know how to make it if you didn't have any instructions?" Miss Violet asked.

"I didn't have instructions on paper if that's what you're asking. I did have directions, though," Conley replied.

"And how did you get those directions?" Miss Violet asked.

Conley was feeling a bit cornered. He nervously looked over at Special Agent Henry. "Where are we going with all these questions?"

Miss Violet started laughing. "You can fool the CIA with any answer you want to throw out there but you can't fool the one that sent you the directions while you slept."

Conley's eyes opened wide and a gasp escaped his mouth. "You're the one that sent me that dream?"

Miss Violet smiled, "Yes, I'm your grandmother, Violet. I haven't seen you since you were a youngster. Now that I have introduced myself in my own special way we can talk. I've come to spend part of the day with you before I have to leave and go help the CIA. Did you know there's a war over oil starting across the ocean? I don't think white men can get along with anyone. The CIA has learned my dreams can help but I can't talk about that. I'll help because it'll save the lives of many Native Americans that serve our country."

"May I get you both some coffee?" Conley asked.

"Tea for me will do just fine," Miss Violet said.

"What about you, Special Agent Henry?" Conley asked.

"Coffee, black," Special Agent Henry said.

"I hope you like history, Conley. I've come so I can pass down what I know about our family. I don't want it lost and forgotten," Miss Violet said.

Conley hurried and prepared the coffee and tea and brought it over and handed it to his guests. He sat down next to Miss Violet and said, "I'm very interested. So please begin."

Miss Violet started, "My grandfather, called Strong Spear, and his brother fought in a battle called Little Big Horn. Chief Sitting Bull had seen in a vision or dream that a mass of Indians defeated Custer. He then gathered the largest group of Indians ever known at one time and when Custer moved in to kill them they over ran Custer killing him and all of his men. It was at a great cost to the Indians too and many died including my father's brother, Angry Bear. After that they were then being hunted and that's when Chief Sitting Bull moved his tribe into Canada rather than to give up and be moved to a reservation. Canada granted them asylum from the United States. I have relatives still living in Canada today."

"So, Chief Sitting Bull had the dreams?" Conley asked.

"Yes, there was a secret dream society that many Lakota belonged to and many in the dream society were our relation." Miss Violet took a sip of her tea.

"Tell me more about the dreams," Conley said.

"First I must tell about our family history. Chief Red Cloud was a Lakota chief and was one of my distant cousins. He was the only main chief to sign the treaty giving away the Indian's rights to the Black Hills. He did this because his people were starving to death when Chief Red Cloud had to lead them onto the reservation. Because of that the government took the Black Hills, or Paha Sapa it is called in Lakota, anyway, the government took it away from the Indians. But the actual treaty said that all the main chiefs had to sign and with Chief Red Cloud being the only main chief that did the Native Americans of today fought the government over the rights to the Black Hills and won. The government offered them money in exchange for the property but the Indians wanted the sacred land instead of money. Today, both the Lakota Indians and the United States Government claim the Black Hills with the government still having control over the land."

"Did you live in the Black Hills?" Conley asked.

"I was born in the Paha Sapa. A long time ago the Black Hills belonged to the Lakota and white men were not supposed to go into that area according to the Fort Laramie Treaty of 1868 but once gold was found in the mountains six years later neither the Calvary nor the Indians could keep them out. The gold rush was on and more and more white men moved into the sacred land belonging to the Lakota people," Miss Violet said.

Conley had pulled out a note book and was writing down some notes. He thought this was worth putting down on paper to remember. He saw a red eight pointed star on Miss Violet's homemade deer skin shoulder bag that looked very much like the star on the horse blankets in his dream. He had to ask, "What's that star on your purse, Miss Violet?"

"That's the symbol on our nation's flag. It reminds me of how badly our people were treated back then and are still treated today."

"Grandma, I mean Miss Violet, does our dreams make us fortune tellers, you know, soothsayers?" Conley asked.

"Nay, not at all. A soothsayer reads bad energies and we just have dreams that can come true. Sometimes the results may be the same. And before you ask, we are not prophets either. Prophets deal with future energies. Again sometimes the results can be the same. We dream about things that help people and not in the energies that are bad or from the future. There is a difference," Miss Violet said.

Conley was thinking and taking every word in as Miss Violet continued.

"At the battle of Wounded Knee the Seventh Calvary division, after the defeat of General Custer, was leading a bunch of the Lakota people to the reservation post at Pine Ridge. The Indians that were captured were mostly all old and sick Indians. The rest of the people were women and children. All of them were starving and freezing to death and in no shape to offer any resistance to the soldiers.

"At Wounded Knee, which is only a dozen or so miles from the Pine Ridge Agency, the army attacked the Indians. They used cannon fire filled with nails to kill almost all of our people. Hundreds of helpless and unarmed Indians died. Women and children and old men and sick Indians lay dead or dying on the frozen snow covered earth at Wounded Knee. Only a few Indians got away and the few left that were still alive were taken on to the Pine Ridge Agency where just a few of those lived. I had a great aunt named Lily that died that day and one of the babies that died was another distant cousin. Her name was Yellow Iris. I am partial to relatives with flower names." Miss Violet smiled.

"Miss Violet, is there any recorded history of our family?" Conley asked.

"Nah, we always kept track by telling stories. If it were written down it would just read like the Bible with pages of who begot whom. I don't have that much time today to tell you all the stories. Today I just wanted you to know about some of your history.

"Like about Chief Crazy Horse and how Chief Crazy Horse had many dreams or visions. One of Chief Crazy Horse's dreams was that no white man would ever kill him. He had ridden and fought against many soldiers and most of the times he was out numbered. His name, Crazy Horse, came from being able to ride his horse in a crazy way in which no one else could have done in battle.

"Later Chief Crazy Horse was stabbed and died at the hands of another Indian which was working for the army as a scout, not by a white man. Chief Crazy Horse was one of the Oglala Lakota chiefs under Chief Sitting Bull that led the charge against General Custer at Little Big Horn. Chief Crazy Horse was close to our family. We had many uncles and cousins that rode with him and died for him."

"It sounds like all of our ancestors had the dreams," Conley said.

"Not all, but many did. It was more common back then than it is now. I'll tell of one more important part of our history before I go. I'm getting tired and still need to stop and see your mom for a few minutes while I'm able.

"Black Elk had visions or dreams that guided him along the way. He was a holy man or medicine man, Shaman if you will, of the Oglala Lakota nation and was second cousin to Crazy Horse, also an Oglala Lakota Indian. Black Elk had been taken to England and when he returned his family had moved and a dream or vision had guided him to find them once he was back. He had dreams that showed him where the buffalo were and that gave the people food. He used his dreams to heal others."

"You can use dreams to heal others?" Conley asked.

"Yes, one can dream what is wrong and what it takes to fix that problem. Usually only experienced dreamers can do that and usually can only do it for someone they are related to," Miss Violet said.

"Tell me more about Black Elk," Conley said.

"I've heard that he dreamed about Wounded Knee and was trying to get there to warn them. He heard the shots being fired but by the time he arrived it was too late.

"There were several marriages between his family and ours. He was family to us." Miss Violet stopped and took her fingers and tapped the drum once more. "It has a good sound."

"Thank you."

Miss Violet stood up and walked half way to the door and stopped. She turned and looked Conley in the eyes and said, "I have to go now. I wanted you to know where you came from. I think maybe you felt lost growing up and now you are not lost. Now you can be proud of our family. You can be proud of who you are."

Conley moved forward and gave Miss Violet a hug. "Thank you for coming to talk with me. I'll always remember this day."

"Do you know what the word Lakota means to us?" she asked.

"No, I don't," Conley said.

"It means human being."

Miss Violet smiled then just left without saying good-bye.

Conley was beginning to realize the connection of his dreaming episodes and this Oglala tribe. He returned to his computer and clicked on another link. He saw a picture that made his heart skip a beat. It was a present-day picture of an old Native American woman and the page was one from a church on the Pine Ridge Reservation asking for help for the elderly.

The older Native Americans were in need of fuel oil for heating their houses. Over the last few years several older Native Americans had died during the harsh winters from not having heat and this church was raising money to see that this didn't happen again. The lady in the picture was helping to raise money and looked very much like the old Indian lady in his dream.

He found out her name was Rose Oneshoe and she lived on the Pine Ridge Reservation. That was all the information listed about the old lady. Conley felt he could get more information by contacting the church. There was no address for the church only a phone number to call if you wanted to donate money for the fuel oil fund so Conley called the toll free number.

Conley explained how he found the number and asked about the lady called Rose. The voice on the other end was confused and wanted to know how much money he could send them. They wouldn't say anything about the ad or the church or give out any information about Rose. They acted as if they never heard of her and only wanted money.

After going around and around with them for several minutes and even asking to speak with someone else, he got nowhere. The conversation always ended up with how much money he was going to donate. He wondered if it could be a scam. He hoped that it was a good organization that did help the people needing it but they weren't able to help him, so after forty minutes of trying he hung up.

Conley spent much of the day researching history of the Oglala tribe and was seriously considering a trip out west to visit the reservation and see if he could locate this woman. He thought with some planning he may get to go for a few weeks in June which he found out was the start of the powwow season. He would enjoy that since he used to dance at some of the local Native American councils in and around where he lived.

Now that he thought for sure he was going to South Dakota, he sat back down at the computer and looked for places and things he would want to do on his trip. It looked like South Dakota had it all. The Oglala Lakota people lived there and the powwows were there. He wanted to see Mount Rushmore. He wanted to camp and hike in the Black Hills and explore the Bad Lands. There were many caves and mines to visit. He wanted to spend a day in Custer State Park. He would also have to fish in several of the lakes stocked with trout. There were many museums he wanted to visit. There were hot air balloon rides or helicopter rides over the Black Hills. He may even be able to take in a rodeo. He saw fields of sun-flowers that went for miles and miles. Now this wasn't a tourist site but they were so beautiful that he didn't want to miss it. He felt even if he could stay a month he would still not see it all.

He saw pictures of all the wild life in that area and would definitely take his camera. There were animals he had only seen on TV such as elk, buffalo, antelope, big horn sheep and mountain goats. There were lots of smaller animals too, like prairie dogs and porcupines.

He loved hunting but not with a gun. His camera was his weapon of choice. He could shoot the animal and have his eight by ten trophy and the animal still had its life and never know it had been shot.

He saw the closest town to fly into was Rapid City so he checked that out too. From there he could rent a car and drive into the Black Hills and Custer State Park. He found a spot in Rapid City where he could camp by a lake and fish. He would love doing that.

In just the one day at the computer his mind was made up. He was going. It is like when he went to look at new cars telling himself that he didn't need one and wasn't going to buy one but in truth he was already sold and just had to find the right one. He knew this about himself and accepted it. Today his right 'car' was the Oglala tribe and the Pine Ridge Reservation. He knew after one day of hearing from his grandmother and seeing all of what South Dakota offered he was sold.

Conley had always enjoyed going places alone. But this time it was different. He was uneasy about going and wanted company. He couldn't wait to ask Emily to go with him.

# CHAPTER 5

Conley and Emily were on their way to a favorite sea food eatery they both enjoyed. This restaurant was built to look like a ship. You entered by walking down a dock with pilings and huge ropes holding the ship in place then walked across a little bridge walkway going over some water to enter. Conley always thought it looked more like a tug boat instead of a ship.

On his drive there he had to stop at a four-way stop where a small framed short lady in an orange vest walked out into traffic and held up a red hand held stop sign. Once all the cars were stopped she allowed the children to cross and watched them as they made it across the street safely where they were on their way home from school.

It was the last day of school for this school year and all the children were very excited. Conley watched as they yelled and threw paper wads at each other.

Conley waved to the crossing guard lady known as Shorty. She waved back and then allowed Conley's Jeep to go first. Politeness had its advantages. Conley smiled and gave her thumbs up as he passed by in appreciation.

When Conley and Emily got to the red painted, tug boat looking restaurant and went inside they walked past a couple waitresses dressed as sailors wearing white round navy Dixie Cup hats like Popeye used to wear.

On the walls were pictures of whales and sharks. In the center of the restaurant was a large aquarium filled with fish like black and white striped angel fish, spotted tiger fish and the orange and white striped clown fish.

They found a table near the window and Emily asked, "So, you're going next week to South Dakota?"

Conley pushed Emily's seat in and then went around the table and sat in his chair. "Yes, I still have to call the airlines and reserve my ticket but before I did that I wanted to ask one more time if you would go with me."

"I wished I could. But like I said when you called the other day, I can't get off work for that long, not right now. And don't worry about your trailer. I will stop by and get your mail and water your potted palm tree and keep an eye on the place while you're gone," she replied. Then she asked, "Do you have anything I have to pay while you are away?"

"I don't think so. I've paid all my bills for the next two months so all should be okay," was his answer.

"The next two months?" Emily's eyebrows arched. "Are you going to be gone that long? I thought you were just going for a few weeks."

"No, just going for a couple weeks, I think. It may take longer. I just paid everything ahead and that way I don't have to worry about anything when I return is all," he replied. "Oh, and I have already paid a neighborhood boy to mow the yard when it needs it."

"I could've done that for you. I like working in the yard and flower gardens," she told Conley.

"You need the extra money that bad?" he teased.

"No, but while you're gone I may set you out a few flowers if you don't mind."

"Sure, I love flowers but you don't have to unless you want to. I'm just glad you're watching out for my place."

"So this is a thank you dinner?" she asked.

"No, you haven't done anything yet," Conley chuckled. "The 'thank you' dinner will be once I get back if you take in my mail," and with that he laughed out loud.

"Oh, you know I will, goofus."

"I know. I was just hoping you could go with me. I love to travel so maybe you can go on a trip with me here soon," Conley said.

"I would like that too," she said as the waitress came to take the order.

Emily ordered the coconut covered shrimp and Conley got the stuffed flounder and an order of crab cakes for appetizers.

"I'll miss seeing you at the casino. You've been there a lot lately," Emily said.

"Yep, I had to go more often than I usually do to make enough money to go on this trip plus I had to get all the bills paid ahead. Now if anything comes up you have my number and I'll be calling you when I can just to make sure you are okay."

"Why are you flying instead of driving out?" she asked.

"It took me awhile to decide but I'm going to fly then rent a car once there. I figured that would be faster and the extra luggage and car rental wouldn't be that much more. I only have one suitcase of clothes and a duffel bag with a small tent and some camping gear and my fishing tackle. I am not sure what I'll need but once I get somewhere I usually manage," he answered.

"Did you find out any more information about that Indian woman, the one in the dream you are trying to track down?"

"No, I hope to run her down once there and at least get to talk with her. But I'm not sure I'll even find her. All I can do is try."

"What's so important about you finding this Indian lady in your dream anyway?" Emily asked.

"Emily, I have a problem I need your advice on. I grew up with the dreams and at the time they were very confusing to me when I was young. Hell, they still confuse me. But now my twin daughters are having the dreams and I don't know how to help them. I feel lost as to what I can do for them. I was hoping the lady in the dream was my grandmother but she isn't. My grandmother

Violet came to see me to tell me of my Indian ancestors. So, at least now I know that the dream lady isn't my grandmother. I have to find out what I can about the dreams for my daughters sake. Am I being silly and wasting my time with this trip? I really don't know what else to do."

"No, I don't think you are. Sounds like you need someone to guide you with your dreams. Maybe this lady is your native dream guide," Emily responded.

"I never thought about that. I hope you're right. Thanks, that makes me feel better."

"What did your mother say about the Indian woman's picture you copied and showed to her? Did she know who she might be?" Emily wanted to know.

"She took the picture and looked it over real good. I told her the lady's name and she sat up and said that was an Indian name. She didn't give me much more than that. She doesn't like me digging up that area of her life. I don't know what went on back then so I just have to respect her wishes and feelings about it all," Conley answered.

The food arrived and Conley caught himself just watching Emily as she started eating. Her pleasant looking thin face and the way she wore her hair enchanted Conley. She looked up and Conley blinked then grabbed his fork and looked down to his plate.

"Maybe I'll gain some understanding how it was for my mom when she lived on the reservation. It would help me understand myself more, you know, from being raised from her point of view. Even though we may sometimes disagree with what we were taught as a child we still reflect those ideals in the way we think and act as an adult. So whatever I learn on this trip should be interesting," Conley said.

"That's very true. I've found out that I have some guilt that stems from the way I was raised as a child that doesn't even have anything to do with me now or then for that matter. It was just passed down to me from a parent and as a kid I just accepted it as part of who I am.

"After growing up I found out that some of the way I feel about myself stems from those early feelings and really doesn't have too much to do with who I really am. But if we don't realize all this at some point then we continue believing and acting in that old way for absolutely no good reason.

"Most of us reject our earlier upbringing but what we should do is just try and understand how we were raised and make a judgment to evaluate ourselves to see if how we feel and act is true to who we are or if we are merely reacting to how we were raised and what we were taught. One way we keep repeating the process without knowing it and the other way we can identify and change who we are and what we want to be.

"Listen at me; I am talking away as if I was one of my college professors." Emily flushed.

"Hey, that makes perfect sense to me. We all have choices but if we don't know what the choices are then it's like only having one choice so that's what we continue doing. But when we are shown a different way or better way, you know, have a better understanding of what's what, then we become aware of the choices and can pick something more fitting for our life. Life is about choices. But if we continue making the same choice that doesn't work we'll get the same results we always got and never change anything." Conley paused then asked, "What could you possibly feel guilt about?"

"Well, to start with, I was born a girl. My dad wanted a boy and no matter how much of a tomboy I tried to be it wasn't the same, it wasn't good enough. And the truth is I never made a very good tomboy either," Emily chuckled.

"Well, I'm sure glad you didn't," Conley answered. It was moments like this that Conley was pleased with having a friend like Emily. Her beauty on the inside matched what one could see on the outside. She could talk of things other than a job or a television show. Conley knew she had her own thoughts and ideas not just ideas she heard somewhere that she passed on as her own to be cool or fit in. Conley thought she didn't need to show off for others because she had an acceptance of herself.

Emily pulled up and parked her car in front of the airline terminal that Conley would be flying out of in about an hour. She got out and opened the trunk and helped Conley with his suitcase and duffel bag. He set them on the corner of the sidewalk and they held each other's hands a moment then hugged.

Conley was torn. His head wanted to go and find out what he could about the lady in his dream but his heart wanted to stay and be with Emily. He was already missing her and he hadn't even left yet.

"Well, you stay safe and come back in one piece," Emily said after holding onto him for a few minutes.

"I will. I really need to go and do this but at the same time I wish I could stay or that you could've gone with me. I usually go places to just enjoy being somewhere new and exciting but this time it feels different. It doesn't feel like a pleasure trip but more like, umm, taking a final exam for a college class or something. I guess I'm excited about going but at the same time I dread it too for some reason," he returned.

"Well, don't worry about me or anything here. All will turn out okay and you'll be back home before you even know it. Now give me one last hug and be on your way before the plane leaves without you," Emily said.

Conley gave her another hug and a kiss on the cheek then picked up his luggage and headed for the check in counter. Emily got back into her car and drove off waving.

*The Indian lady is riding her pony very fast and motions for Conley to hurry. He can hear the galloping sound of the horse's hooves. He sees sweat forming on the pony's neck. He feels like he is flying after her but can't catch up to her no matter how fast he is going. The pony heads down a pass between two rock walls. When Conley flies down that path he feels the tree branches hit his right shoulder. Again the branches from the trees hit his shoulder and this time he opens his eyes.*

He raised his head up from the tray in front of him not knowing where he was for a second. The stewardess shook his shoulder again and told him the plane was landing in Minneapolis and he had to return his seat and tray to the upright position and fasten his seat belt.

As he departed the plane he was going to visit a shop or two before his next flight took off. He landed at gate two and thought it best to visit some shops closer to where his next plane boarded. He checked his ticket. He had an hour before the next plane left but it was leaving out of gate 104 so he headed for the other end of the airport.

Conley got on one of those slow moving sidewalks and allowed it to take him down the corridors toward where he caught his change over flight. It was slow and he kept checking his watch and watching how far he had come. After thirty-five minutes he was still only a little over half way there so he had to get off the moving sidewalk and hurry along the corridors at a faster pace if he was going to make it on time.

When he arrived at gate 104 the plane was already boarding. It was a good thing he didn't visit any shops at the other end of the airport or he would have missed his flight. Was the old Indian lady telling him to hurry for that reason or was there something else he had to hurry for once he got to South Dakota?

# CHAPTER 6

T he plane going into Rapid City was a smaller plane and Conley could see everyone on board from where he sat. There was one Native American man about thirty years old ahead of him and he wanted to say hello but didn't get the chance.

The plane landed and Conley got his bags and was looking for a taxi to take him into Rapid City to the camping spot he had found on the Internet. This spot had the fishing lake and Conley thought this would be a good place to start.

The Native American man came up to Conley and spoke, "Hi, where're you headed?"

"I'm just going to grab a taxi out front and go to the campground over by a lake."

"Where are you from?" the Native American man asked.

"The largest city close to me is Indianapolis," Conley answered.

"Ah, land of the Shawnee."

"I saw you on the plane but didn't get a chance to say hello. My name is Conley and I'm out here to see if I can find a lady called Rose Oneshoe. You haven't heard of her by chance?" he asked as he offered up a hand shake.

"Hmm, nay, don't think so. By the way my name is Longknife and I'm an artist. I just got back from Chicago where I painted a giant Indian mural in the lobby of a hotel. I'll have to go back and paint another one next month. I'm excited, if you can't tell. This was my first really big commissioned job, my dream job, but you wouldn't understand about that. Let me give you a ride and I only ask because you look more Indian than white. Are you FBI?"

"Do I look like I'm FBI? I'm not carrying a gun or wearing a badge," Conley said.

"Nay, not that kind of FBI. FBI as in full blooded Indian. You must be at least half," Longknife chuckled.

"Are you FBI?" Conley asked.

"Yep, been that way my whole life." Longknife had a big grin on his face.

"It sounds pretty cool to be FBI. Is there a difference?" Conley asked.

"Well, in a way I guess. Off rez it isn't much different. Indian is Indian. But on rez there are some resentment between FBI and half breeds. Sometimes the half breeds get the government jobs more so than the FBI. Never figured out why. That's just how it is. Now, how about that ride?" Longknife replied.

Longknife was a lean muscular man in his late twenties to early thirties. He had dark skin and very high cheek bones. His hair was long, black and shiny. He wore his hair down and had a braided leather head band across his forehead to keep his hair out of his eyes.

Conley felt pleased that Longknife had offered him a ride and also befriended him since he looked somewhat Native American. This was a good start to the trip. "Sure, a ride would be great. I can pitch in a little gas money. Do you know where the camping ground by the lake is?"

"Yeah, it isn't much out of my way," Longknife said as they walked to his truck.

On the way to the campground Conley asked a lot of questions. He needed to know where he could find out about Rose and how to meet the right people that may know about her.

"Well," said Longknife, "There's a powwow here in Rapid in a few days down at the convention center. You can start there. Just go up and talk to as many Indians as you can and maybe someone there will have at least heard of her."

"May I ask how you got the name Longknife?" Conley asked.

"A long time ago when the Indians first had to come to the reservations they had to give a name. Many only had one name so the guard there usually took a look and then added the last name. My ancestor carried a very long knife, maybe a Calvary sword so he was called Longknife. Okay, looks like we're here," he answered as he pulled his truck off the road and down a short lane to a camping area with a lake not far from where the tents and campers were located.

Conley got out and thanked Longknife for the ride and conversation. "Good luck," Longknife said as he started to leave.

"Oh, wait. Will I see you at the powwow?" Conley asked.

"Nah, I am headed home after being gone for a few weeks. I live down on the rez just outside the town of Pine Ridge," was the reply. "You take care." And he drove away.

Conley went into the office and rented a space to put up his tent. The people there were very kind and helpful telling him about the layout of the area and what all there was to do. He got a time the bus stopped by about five blocks away and they went over the laws regarding fishing and the usual tourist and sightseeing information for the area.

He spent the next hour putting up his small tent and arranging his camp area and was now hungry. He wanted to catch his dinner from the lake but needed a fishing license first. He was told if he followed the creek up about a mile there was a hatchery where he could get a license and information about how to catch the trout stocked in the lake here at the campground. So he set out hiking up Rapid Creek.

He had not gone far when he ran across a rather large deer. She was beautiful and allowed Conley to get close to her. She circled in front of him and as he kept moving along the path then she would again cut in front of him and move off in a direction away from the creek. He took out his camera and got several good close up shots of this deer.

She again moved in front of him and repeated the same move or action. As he got further along the path the deer bolted and ran across a meadow with tall grass. Conley then saw why the deer moved in front of him and was trying to lead him away from that area. As the deer ran through the tall grass a baby fawn was running to catch its mom.

At first all Conley could see was the tall grass parting. The fawn would jump high enough to see where the mom deer was running toward and head in that direction. Soon the baby would jump again to spot the mom and try to run in her direction to catch her. The mom headed for some trees and was soon out of sight. The baby jumped one more time to spot its mom and then also found the tree line and both were gone and now safe.

Conley was in awe of how Mother Nature protected its creatures and how the mother deer looked out for its baby. He had never seen anything like this back home in Indiana.

A few minutes later he came upon the fish hatchery and went inside. Inside he saw the lobby was set up as an information station. There were lots of lighted pictures on the walls and several displays of how fish grew from the eggs to adults. One of the back walls had stuffed trout on plaques so one could study or see up close how beautiful the fish actually were.

"Hello, can I get a fishing license here?" Conley asked the man wearing a dark green uniform.

"Yes, you sure can," the ranger said. "And you're welcome to tour our hatchery if you would like."

"So, this is what the license money goes for," Conley said.

"Yes, one third of all money collected from licenses and fines are used to replenish and restock the lakes and rivers all over this section of the state. We have people come in from all over the United States to fish here just for that reason."

"How often do you stock the lakes and rivers around here?"

"We stock the area with the trout four times a summer. Most of the fish are between twelve and eighteen inches long and we have a limited amount of the larger fish going with each drop."

Conley wondered why all states didn't do the same thing. He paid for the fishing license and was handed a brochure telling about the fish he could catch.

The ranger said, "You can only keep five trout a day. And please don't use corn as bait. Corn is what we feed some of the ones we turn into the lakes and that wouldn't be fair to the fish."

"One or two a day is plenty for me. I just want a few a day to eat while I'm here. What do the trout here like to eat? What's a good bait to use?" Conley asked.

"Trout hit worms, dough balls, minnows and for artificial bait they hit flies and rooster tails. Trout face the current so you need to cast up stream and let the bait float back down to where you are. That way they see the bait coming to them," the ranger said.

Conley said thanks and walked through the hatchery to see the large tanks holding the fish. There were all sizes of fish. Most were about a foot long but others were twenty to thirty inches long.

He bought a couple handfuls of little pellets from a machine and got to throw them in the tanks and watch as the trout would hit the pellets and swallow them. He leaned down and just put his fingers in the water and sure enough some of the fish would swim right up to him and touch his fingers. It was almost like he got to pet them.

He walked down to the last building and inside was thousands of tiny baby fish or fry. The rangers hatched them in these tanks and kept them inside to protect them from the elements such as weather or birds that would eat them. They fed them a special diet until they were large enough to transfer to the other holding tanks outside.

Conley returned to camp and put together his small fishing pole and grabbed his artificial baits and headed back to where the creek ran into the lake. He cast out and let the current bring the bait back to him.

Conley looked all around and enjoyed seeing the mountains in the background. He was in the foot hills and could see mountains in every direction. He watched as a long black snake slid across the water looking for its meal of minnows or maybe a small frog.

He saw a man fly fishing and watched as the guy made the line go back and forth over his head several times then land the fly in the water clear on the other side of the creek. There was an art to fly fishing and Conley just watched as he had no idea how to fish that way. Conley figured he would have the fly caught in the top of a tree somewhere because he did that more than he wanted to admit just fishing with a rod and reel. When he did end up with his line tangled in a tree Conley usually commented that he was fishing for flying fish.

He lost track of time but then something hit his lure. Conley jerked his pole and watched as the fish made its run and it jumped several times trying to throw the hook from its mouth. It gave a descent fight and when he brought it in he had caught about a two pound trout.

He returned to camp, cleaned the fish and was going to put it on one of the grills the campsite had for use. He noticed the red meat and thought that was strange since he had caught trout before and they weren't red inside. When the fish was cooked he took a bite and noticed how it tasted like salmon and not trout. It was good so he ate it all.

He cleaned up his mess and saw the lady from the office raking up leaves around the campground and asked her why the trout tasted like salmon. She informed him that some of the trout was cross-bred with salmon so they would do better in the wild.

The day was ending with Conley sitting in a lawn chair watching people walk along the lake and throwing bread to the many assortments of ducks the lake attracted and was known for. Tomorrow he would look at the map he obtained from the office and decide what to do next.

*Half-grown baby ducks are running around the water playing. Some are jumping in the water and swimming away from the others. The ducks swim across the water and others are running around the bank and jumping in after them. They are quacking at each other and seem to be having fun.*

*The mother ducks are all together watching their young. Some mother ducks are picking at their feathers and grooming themselves. Once in a while a mother duck will straighten her head up high and look for its young. Once she spots the duckling she then returns to her business of cleaning her feathers.*

*A new duck with a much smaller young duckling arrives. She looks around for a spot to make her comfortable. She is much thinner than most of the other ducks. Her little one is just barely waddling. The baby duck still has its yellow fuzz and hasn't started growing feathers yet.*

*The Mom duck settles in and is getting a drink. The baby duck waddles over to the edge of the water and falls in. The mom loses sight of the baby duck. The little duckling sinks to the bottom. It can't swim.*

The next morning Conley went to the creek and started fishing for his next meal. He had caught a small trout and brought it back to camp for breakfast.

"I'm sorry it is so muggy and hot so early this morning. The humidity is high today. It's at forty percent. It's not usually this high," the lady running the campground said.

"It's hot this morning but I don't mind forty percent humidity. Where I come from that's low. We usually have it in the eighties so for me this isn't bad at all," Conley said.

"Well, if you get too hot you can use our pool any time you wish. It's over behind the office in case you haven't found it yet," the lady said.

"That sound like a great idea. Thanks," Conley said.

Conley finished cleaning up from his breakfast. He was already forming beads of sweat on his forehead. Taking a swim sounded like just the thing he needed.

He hadn't brought any swim trunks so he used a pair of short pants. He grabbed a towel and walked over to the pool.

The pool area was protected with a chain link fence. He opened the gate and walked over to a plastic chair and sat down to take his shoes off.

He noticed several moms were getting tans while the kids played in the water. The kids were running around and jumping in with their feet tucked up under them so when they hit the water next to their friends it would make a big splash. He heard one kid yell, "Cannon ball!" Then the kid would run and jump in to make a small title wave that hit the others. Another kid yelled "Jackknife," as he ran and jumped into the water holding only one knee up to his chest. The jackknife dive made a bigger splash than the cannonball.

Conley saw one very young kid by himself at the end of the pool. His mom was putting suntan lotion on. The little boy couldn't walk very well because he had on one of those little inner tubes. It was yellow and had a duck's head on it.

Conley's heart started pounding faster. He knew he had to be on his toes. Conley remembered the dream.

# CHAPTER 7

Conley watched as the children played and splashed each other. He was watching the little boy with the duck inner tube closely. Everything seemed to be agreeable. He didn't see any danger so far. After all he couldn't just jump up and stop the kid from playing.

Conley walked to the end of the pool and dove in. He swam several laps by swimming around all the other kids that were playing. It felt so refreshing. The temperature of the water was cool but not cold.

A ball was thrown near Conley and he stopped swimming and took the ball and threw it back to the children. He swam another few laps then pulled himself up and sat on the edge of the pool on the far side. He had to wipe the chlorine from his eyes.

Conley was feeling better about his dream. Maybe this pool wasn't the place he had seen in the dream. He looked over to find the little boy wearing the yellow duck.

The mom was reaching for her glass of ice water she had on a table next to her. Conley saw the inner tube floating in the water. He looked around to see where the kid was. He didn't see him but Conley knew where the little boy was.

Conley yelled at the top of his lungs, "Your little baby is in the water! Get him."

Conley stood up and dove into the water to swim where the boy had gone down. The mom looked then jumped in where the little boy's yellow duck was floating.

By the time Conley swam across the pool the mom had the little boy in her arms and was setting him on the side of the pool. Conley helped her lay the boy down while they both got out of the pool and was checking the boy. He wasn't breathing.

The mom used CPR and soon the little boy was spitting up water and crying. The mom held him in her arms.

"Thank you so much," she said.

"You're very welcome. You acted quickly and knew just what to do," Conley said.

"Yes, I'm a doctor. I don't want to sound rude but I want to get him back to our motor home and make sure he is alright. Thank you again," she said.

Conley's eyes got watery as he watched the lady carry the little boy back to their motor home. He didn't understand why he got upset after events were over. After all, everything turned out well and having a few tears had no useful contribution once it was over.

Conley had spent the last two days fishing and hiking. Yesterday he had hiked about four miles up the creek past the fish hatchery and found an old gold mine. The mine held no gold now and there was a small charge to go in so he paid and followed the path into the mine.

In the opening of the mine there was a path to the left and a creek with water running down and out of the mine from the right side. He studied the little creek bed for signs of gold in case the owner had missed seeing one.

At the end of the cave one could see where the water was coming from. They had colored lights at the end shining on a water fall coming through an opening in the roof. It was beautiful and Conley took a lot of pictures. The mine ran underneath Rapid Creek. He had never heard of a waterfall coming out of a dead end mine like this and thought it was very different. The lights took turns coming on to give the waterfall a different look with each color. He got a picture of the waterfall from every color light that shown on it.

Hiking back, he followed the road. He found another attraction not far from the mine just across the street. He went over to check it out. He found a cave this time with a gift shop you had to go through first, of course.

There was an area beside the road where you could park and held the gift shop. Behind that was a ravine with a swinging bridge that went over to the cave that opened up in the side of a huge cliff. He went inside the gift shop to see how much the cost was to explore the cave. He figured it was just a tour through the cave and that was okay with him.

Conley went inside and looked around the gift shop. He ended up talking to the owner working behind the counter. "When is the next tour of the cave?" he asked.

"It's in about ten minutes. So far we have about a dozen people going. Would you like a ticket?" the man asked.

"Yes, did your family find this cave years ago?" Conley asked.

"Oh heavens no. I came here eleven years ago and found this was for sale so I bought it and just stayed. Where are you from?" the man asked.

"I'm from Indiana not too far from Brookville Lake," Conley said.

"Really? I used to live only a few miles north of there. I was groundskeeper over at White Water State Park just a few miles north of Brookville Lake. My daughter is taking the group out the back door now if you will please join them. Enjoy your tour," the man said.

"Thank you, I will."

Conley thought with the country being as big as it was the population seemed small. He remembered running into neighbors quite often on his trips like he did today.

He took the tour with ten or twelve others and found out, from the tour guide, that Jesse James had hidden in this very cave. Of course he knew that all attraction like this had to have some really neat historic value to tell the visitors even if it wasn't true and that made the visit more thrilling and exciting.

It only took forty to fifty minutes to go through the cave. The inside was pretty and worth seeing. Conley was on the lookout for crystals but this cave didn't have any. The group was shown several stalactites hanging down from the roof and the matching stalagmites below them.

At one part the cave opened up into a large room called the Ball Room. The group entered the Ball Room from what looked to be the second level or balcony. There were rocks that formed a railing where people could stand and look down to the other part of the room below. In the center of this rock railing were rock steps leading down to one side of the main room.

The Ball Room was fairly flat and at the far end was what looked to be a rock podium. On each side of this podium were rather large rock chairs looking much like a throne for a king and queen. There were lights that spotlighted the throne chairs to make them stand out.

The group was told someone famous once had a wedding there. A duke from Great Britain visited the area once and came back later with his bride to be. He had a small wedding party and even though the party was small for a wedding it filled the Ball Room of the cave to its capacity.

They were all dressed in tuxedoes and formal gowns. The priest stood at the podium and the groom and bride sat in the throne chairs for the ceremony.

They even brought three violins players who stood above on the balcony. They played music and everyone danced in the Ball Room as best as they could with the room they had.

Conley thought that would be different. Maybe someday he could do something like that for his wedding if he ever found anyone that could put up with him. He chuckled to himself as that thought ran cross his mind.

Today Conley had caught the bus and was heading downtown to the convention center to go to the powwow. He watched out the window as the bus went through the sections of town along its route. The neighborhoods looked like any other neighborhoods in just about any city he had been to. He could have been anywhere in the United States but he enjoyed the ride just the same.

The bus stopped at a Native American history museum and the driver told Conley this was as close to the convention center as he could go without having to change buses. The driver pointed to where the convention center was just over the railroad tracks across the main road they were on.

Conley got out and said thanks then looked around. He went in to check out the history museum. It had a lot of information about the Oglala tribe and he met several people from that tribe inside.

"Hello, my name is Conley. How are you today?" he said to one young lady standing with her daughter looking at one of the exhibits.

"Hi, I'm Terri and this is my three year old, Demi. Have you come to go to the powwow?" she asked.

"Yes, have you been over there yet?"

"Nay, this powwow is mostly for tourist and to make money. It's what they call a competition powwow. People at this powwow dance to win money. It's still worth seeing if you haven't been to one though," Terri said.

"Okay, thanks. What are the other kinds of powwows?"

"Well, the traditional powwow is one that is used for our religious ceremonies. There's one of those starting this coming weekend. It's a seven day powwow," Terri said.

"I would love to see that one. Where's the traditional one going to be held?" Conley asked.

"It'll be down on the rez at Porcupine. It's more for Indians but visitors are welcome too," Terri said.

Conley spent a few minutes talking to Terri and meeting her three year old daughter. They were both very shy talking to someone they didn't know.

"Will I see you at the powwow in Porcupine?" Conley asked.

"Yeah, we're goin' to that one. I live in Porcupine."

"Would you two like to go over to the powwow today with me?" Conley asked.

"Nay, we're waiting for someone."

"Okay, I'm going to head on over then. I hope to see you next week at the powwow in Porcupine," Conley said.

"Bye and have fun," Terri said.

Conley left to head across the railroad tracks to the convention center to see the powwow being held there.

The convention center was a good sized place. There were lots of cars, trucks, and campers in the parking lot which was almost full. He saw many cars and vans with the doors open and people getting on their colorful outfits and many outfits were full of feathers. It reminded him of when his daughters were in beauty pageants and had to dress and change outfits for the different competitions when they were little only they didn't use the feathers.

Conley's heart was racing with excitement. He had danced at a few Native American councils in and around where he lived back in Indiana but they usually only had a few dancers with only one or two of those dancers being real Native Americans. It was nothing like this.

Once inside he had to go into the grandstand to sit. The grandstands were only about half full. Most of the people there were on the floor dancing.

The floor only allowed the dancers to enter and there were many. The floor was almost full of dancers. At one end of the floor were the drums and singers. The announcer told that there was over one hundred dancers and announced what each dance meant and introduced each drum group. There were dancers from many different states and drum and singing groups from many of the different reservations in and across that part of the United States.

Conley looked around and spotted a Native American family to sit beside. He hoped that one of the young men could tell him what was going on and explain the different dances to him.

Conley introduced himself, "Hi, I'm Conley. I'm from Indiana. How are you all doing today?"

"Hello, I'm called Owl. It's good to meet you."

"Is Al short for Albert?"

"No, it's short for Spotted Owl, my family name."

"Ah, okay."

The announcer called for all dancers to go to the east end of the dancing ring.

"Why are all the dancers lining up like that?" Conley asked.

"First there's a progression of all the dancers to enter the arena from the east called the Grand Entry. They move around the arena in a circle and once all the dancers are in they stop to allow the medicine man to say a prayer. After that is the color guard. Some of the elders present the flags of the different Native American Nations that are represented here today. Then comes the South Dakota state flag and the United States flag and they are set in a stand in the center of the circle to remain there the rest of the day," Owl said.

"Oh, it's an opening ceremony. This is so neat. I've never seen anything like this before. I've only seen a few dancers a couple times back home," Conley said.

After the Grand Entry was over the announcer asked for all the grass dancers to enter the ring. Conley watched as these dancers jumped around and stomped.

"What are these dancers doing?" Conley asked.

"These men have on multicolored outfits that have ribbons and yarn hanging down from the outfit that resembles grass. They dance first. They stomped around in a dance move that was used to tromp down all the tall grass in a field where the powwow is going to be held so the others will have a nice flat area to dance. This isn't needed in this arena with a wood floor but it's the tradition and gives people an understanding of how we do things," Owl said.

The men and women danced next. This was the traditional dancers. It was the type dance Conley had done back home. They danced around the circle in a slow step and on the upbeat sections of the songs they held up one hand with a feather for the ladies and a coup stick which is a war club for the men about five or six times to the drum beat.

The announcer called for the shawl dancers.

"This is pretty. The women are exquisite looking as they dance," Conley said. "The shawls they use are very colorful with the orange, yellow, blue and red designs really standing out. I like the fringe along the edges and some I see have colorful ribbons matching the outfits. It's all very beautiful"

"This is a dance for the women called a shawl dance where all the women wear and dance with a shawl. Most of the women have made their own shawls. Now, as you can see, they are being joined with the younger girls that are called jingle dancers. These girls wear dresses made with shiny tin cone shaped ornaments in rows across the dress that jingled when they move. These jingle cones were originally made from the lids of tins that held tobacco back in the pioneer days. These dances are very lively and allow the young girls to show their stuff to attract a male caller," Owl said.

"I see that most of the male dancers wear bells around their ankles. What is that for?"

"The drum beat is the heartbeat of Mother Earth and the vibration comes up from the ground and goes into the dancer as they dance. The bells protect the dancer by stopping any bad energy from entering their body."

"How did powwows get started in the first place?" Conley asked.

"Traditionally a powwow was a gathering of many tribes in the spring or summer. It was used to celebrate and reunite family and friends and was the great social event of the year. This was a time when old friends met and talked and was time to meet new friends and even the possibility of finding a mate for the younger adults," Owl answered.

The announcer called for the veteran's dance. This was a dance to honor all the veterans. It started with any Native American who had served in any branch of the military to come down and dance. Then the announcer asked that anyone that was a veteran to come down to the dance floor and join them. They were very proud of those who served.

Conley said thanks to Owl and went down to dance with the veterans.

After that came an invitational dance. The announcer invited anyone wishing to dance with them to join them. Conley being there for the veterans dance stayed for the invitational dance.

Afterward he went over to stand beside the drums and listen to the singing with a small crowd of their followers or groupies. Most of the songs were sung in the Lakota language so he didn't know the words or meanings of the songs.

One of the songs was sung in English. It was a song about being strong like Mighty Mouse and was a cute song for the children dancers. All the children got out on the floor and gave one heck of a performance. One little guy about four or five years old and dressed with just a red handkerchief hanging down in front over his shorts for his outfit would give any of the adults a run for their money. He really cut a shine and was quite a good little dancer. He jerked and stomped to the drum beat. He had all the moves.

Conley took lots of pictures and enjoyed being part of the activities and listening to the drum groups. He liked the music and bought a CD from most of them.

There were so many different outfits. Some were dressed with a feathered headdress and a feathered bustle. The bustles had a fan of feathers making a circle in the back with a small mirror in the center and had horse hair tips off the end of each feather. Many used a leather vest and some had the loin cloth in front. He saw for a few headdresses deer antlers were added. Many had chest plates worn on their chests made from what looked like bones to protect them from being hit with a hatchet or tomahawk.

A lot of the men wore paint on their faces and those that did had their very own design such as a hand prints or just lines across the face. Some of the lines went across the nose and under the eyes while other lines went from the chin to the nose or down from the eyes to the jaw bone.

The older women had long dresses that came to their ankles and shawls around their shoulders. They had a feather in their hair and most wore their hair in braids. The younger ladies wore dresses that came down to their knees and were more colorful. Many of them had small round shiny arrangements or tiny sea shells to adorn their outfits. Their jewelry was made of silver with turquoise and many wore bracelets made from small colorful beads.

Conley stayed near the drums and singing groups once he was there. He got to talk to several Native Americans that way as there were very few in the stands. Most of the people in the stands were tourists and most the Native Americans were dancing it seemed.

He found out that they danced to win money and that is how some of them made their yearly earnings by following what was called the powwow trail. They went from powwow to powwow to earn or win money that would carry them through the next year.

The powwow lasted until nine that night but Conley had to leave by six to catch the last bus back to where he was camping.

He did get an Indian taco before he headed back. It was pretty good because all he had since he got into South Dakota was trout. The Indian taco was a piece of fry bread made like a very thin pancake about the size of a paper plate and had tomatoes, shredded cheese, re-fried beans, and ground beef on it. You could roll it up into a burrito or just fold it over into a taco. It was filling and he enjoyed the fresh and different taste.

The next day Conley got the bus and headed back into town. This time he was going to rent a car and head up into the Black Hills for some sightseeing before going on to the reservation for the next powwow.

He rented the cheapest car on the lot at the time. It was a Geo Metro. This car was a very small car with only three cylinders. He knew it would be good on gas but he was worried about it climbing the hills in the mountains which the dealer told him the little car would do quite well and he wouldn't be sorry a bit for renting it.

He drove the car back to the campground then grabbed his fishing pole. He wanted to get in more fishing before he left and wasn't sure if he would be back at this camp or not. He walked around the lake and went across a little bridge that went over to a small island in the center of the lake he had spotted the first day he was there.

He caught a few fish and released them back into the lake. He found out that trout had to be returned to the water very quickly after being caught or they would die. One of the fish he released floated to the top instead of swimming off so he saved that fish for his lunch.

There was one spot in the lake at the edge that had wide cement steps going down into the water. This was used by families and kids to go down to the water's edge and throw bread pieces to the ducks. As soon as one child threw a bread crumb into the water all the ducks anywhere close by would swim over to get their share if they could. Conley could see many different kinds of wild ducks and overheard one man say as he pointed to a duck with a red spot that it was a rare duck for this area.

He returned to camp late in the afternoon and after fixing his lunch took his tent down and stopped by the office and thanked them for all the help and information they had given him. He packed up and got a map and headed for the mountains of the Black Hills.

His first stop was to find another campground before it got dark. The one he found was owned by a retired couple and he found a quiet place in the back of the campgrounds next to the forest. He set up camp and then grabbed his fishing pole and was off to a nearby lake or stream to see what he could catch for his supper.

He saw the corner of a lake off in the distance at a bend in the road. Conley parked and followed a tiny stream down to the lake. He could easily step across this stream but noticed when he looked really hard that he could see trout laying in the bottom facing the current. They were hard to spot and were the same color as the gravel in the stream bed. The only way he even spotted one was because it moved as he stepped over the water to the other side. After watching the trout for several minutes he went on down to the lake and found that the corner of the water he saw opened up into a rather large lake.

He fished and hiked around the remainder of the day enjoying being where he was and taking in all the sights he could see. At one point Conley was tired of fishing for trout so he put on one of his bass plugs. Back home in Indiana he fished mostly for bass and thought he would try it here just to do something different.

He was remembering fishing with his dad as a kid. His dad would just use a worm and a bobber to fish. Conley however couldn't sit still and would always walk the bank casting his artificial bait and over the years had learned what bass liked and would hit.

His attention was brought back from the past as he felt a good size tug on the spinner bait he was using as he reeled it past some lily pads. He jerked and the fight was on. He soon saw it was a good size bass when it jumped clear out of the water. It jumped again and again as he reeled it in. He had only seen a fish jump like this on one of those fishing shows on television he like watching. It took several minutes to land this fish because when he thought he had it close enough to pull onto land it took off again and fought some more.

Conley finally got it to the bank and took hold of the fish by grabbing the fish's bottom jaw with his thumb in its mouth. He clamped down on the little bone in the bottom of the fish's mouth and that made the bass stop flopping around. He removed the hook and got his handheld fishing scale and weighted his catch. It was the largest Conley had ever caught weighing in at six and a half pounds. It had fought such a good fight that Conley looked it over then set it back down in the water and wiggled it around until it took off swimming away.

This made Conley's day. It was late so Conley headed back to camp. He stopped by the office and bought a post card and wrote a note to Emily and put it in the mailbox shaped like a stage coach, to go out the next morning. After grabbing a ham salad sandwich and a pop he spent the rest of the day in the campgrounds walking around and talking to others.

Conley couldn't shake the feeling that something was about to happen. He was searching his mind for a dream he may have forgotten.

# CHAPTER 8

*T*he old Indian woman is standing on a knoll overlooking a valley. Beside her is her pony with the blaze on its forehead and she is pointing. Conley looks in the direction she points and sees a gathering of people dressed in outfits at a powwow. There are a few booths selling homemade Indian jewelry and a couple booths selling food.

*The old woman then points in the opposite direction. Very far off he can see a pass between two mountain ranges. As he looks, the pass comes up close as if he were brought forward to see clearer. He sees a trail between the two cliffs and a sign with the words "Dillon Pass."*

*In the pass there is yelling and rocks flying through the air. A fight ensues. He is hit by one of the rocks. Everything goes black.*

When Conley woke and opened his eyes he heard a ruckus. He crawled out of his tent and was hit in the head from something that came from the tree beside the tent. It was an acorn and a very angry squirrel was chattering loudly at him. It seemed that the squirrel did not like the fact that Conley had camped where he did.

Conley talked softly to the squirrel and after a few more acorns hit him, the squirrel came down the tree and faced Conley as if it was going to attack and it was barking its disapproval. The little squirrel's tail would jerk up as it told Conley off. The little squirrel turned its back to Conley and with its back feet scratched dirt at Conley.

Conley noticed that a common house cat was making its way toward the squirrel. It had crawled on its belly within a couple yards from the squirrel. The squirrel turned and saw the cat. Both animals froze. The cat started shifting its weight back and forth on its front paws getting ready to pounce.

At that exact moment the squirrel jumped and landed on top of the cat's head knocking the cat's head down into the grass. The cat just sat there confused as the squirrel ran over to the next tree and climbed to safety. This surprised Conley and he had a deeper respect for the squirrel after that move.

The squirrel then climbed to a branch where it could keep an eye on Conley as it calmed down. Every once in a while it would chatter at Conley again to just let him know he hadn't forgotten that Conley was there and that Conley had camped under its tree and that was unforgivable.

After a breakfast of stale corn chips and a Coke, Conley drove over to Sylvan Lake. Sylvan Lake was one of the most beautiful spots Conley had ever been. He instantly fell in love with this park.

The lake water was dark blue in color and there were huge rocks as big as two story farm houses all around. One huge rock was out in the lake and people were swimming over to the rock. There were hiking paths that went in all directions and Conley sat for a long time just taking in everything he saw before he even got out of the car.

He walked around the lake exploring and fishing though he didn't get a bite it was still okay. He followed a path and found a small cave that didn't go very far back into the rocks but the children playing there were having the time of their lives. He felt like one of them.

He followed a path on across the terrain for an hour or two. The path was slowly going up and went through a pine tree forest. The further he went along the path the steeper the path got. The path went behind the Cathedral Spirals rock formation which was the first consideration for the Presidents' heads that is now known as Mount Rushmore. The path ended up at Harney

Peak. Harney Peak is the highest point in South Dakota and the highest point in the United States east of the Rocky Mountains at an elevation of 7,244 feet. He didn't even know that was where he was headed to until he got there.

There were several people there which surprised him since he only saw one other person on the trail coming back toward Sylvan Lake. Maybe there was a shorter path the other people had followed.

He climbed to the top of the stone fire tower and could see far off in all directions. He bet he could see maybe eight or ten different states from where he stood, it was so high.

He saw something that looked like a sheep over off the pathway next to some jagged rocks and asked a guy next to him if that was a big horn sheep.

"No, actually that is a mountain goat, they look like sheep and a big horn sheep looks more like a goat," was the reply.

"Oh," said Conley surprised. "You must live around here."

"Yes, I live north of Rapid in Sturgis where they have the big motorcycle rally every year in July. We came down for a few days just to enjoy nature and relax, you know, get the kids out of the house and away from their computer games," was the reply as he pointed over to his wife and two kids who were climbing around at the base of the stone fire tower.

"What's that Indian doing sitting over on those rocks over there?" Conley asked as he pointed to the other side.

"He's on a vision quest. This place was where Black Elk had his visions. It is common place for a young Indian man to go on a vision quest as a rite of passage. There's a ceremony that includes a vision quest that they must go on to become an adult or warrior."

"If I may ask, do you know what the ceremony is like?" Conley wanted to know.

"Sure, no problem. First they have to purify their body by fasting. Then they go to a sweat lodge. That's to say they go into a covered round tent and hot rocks are brought in and water poured over the rocks to make steam and that allows one to sweat out the impurities. Prayers are said and then the person can go on a vision quest for several days. He then must tell the holy man or medicine man what he saw or experienced so the holy man can explain what he perceived," came the acknowledgment.

"Okay, thanks a bunch," Conley said as the man waved to his wife and started back down the tower to meet with her and the children.

Conley explored around the fire tower. It was like a mini-fort with rock walls and rock steps part of the way up. It was small and had only a few rooms inside. There was a metal set of steps on up to the top where one could look out and see for miles in all directions.

On the way back to Sylvan Lake Conley heard a crashing of something coming through the leaves and branches of some tree not far from him. He froze. He then spotted a bald eagle that had landed on a log only a couple yards from him. Conley didn't move, just watched.

The eagle had walked down the log to the end and was peering into the end of the hollow log he stood on. A little ground squirrel or chipmunk stuck its head out the other end of the log and was watching the eagle. The eagle then spotted the chipmunk. He hopped and halfway ran, waddling almost like a duck, with its wings folded into its side. It ran over to the end of the log to try and get the chipmunk. Soon a chipmunk head popped up through a hole in the top of the log and was watching the eagle.

The bald eagle was a large bird almost the size of a turkey. Conley could see its orange colored beak and the white feathers about its head giving the head an almost bald look and that is how it got its name. It had black wing feathers and the tail feathers were black with white on the ends of the feathers. It had smaller feathers around its legs and orange feet with huge, sharp talons.

This went on for several minutes. The eagle was after the chipmunk and the chipmunk stayed out of its reach and ran inside the log from end to end to see where the eagle was. The eagle went from end to end on top of the log hoping to snatch food for dinner while the dinner or chipmunk kept out of reach and ran inside the log sticking its head out of the far end to keep an eye on the eagle. It reminded Conley of a cartoon and he almost laughed out loud.

At one point the eagle was at one end of the log and the chipmunk ran through the hollow log to the other end and stood on its hind legs. It stretched its front little feet up and grabbed a hold of the top of the log and pulled itself up, with its hind feet dangling off the ground. Doing a chin up it looked to see over the log and check to find where the eagle had landed. Its front feet slipped off and it fell back to the ground and scrambled back into the log before the eagle could waddle and hop to that end of the log to catch it.

Conley tried to raise his camera ever so slowly to get a picture of all this but as soon as he moved the camera up to his eye, the eagle saw the movement and took flight back up through the leaves and branches into the sky and was gone.

The chipmunk came up on top of the log with his two front paws and head up looking at Conley as if to say thanks or maybe just to say who the heck are you? Conley took his picture and the chipmunk watched as Conley went on down the path back to Sylvan Lake.

Later that day Conley drove over to visit Mount Rushmore. On the road near the park he spotted a mom and dad and a baby of what looked like sheep grazing on grass just off the roadway. This time he knew it was mountain goats so now he had seen a family of mountain goats and a big horn sheep. It was really thrilling to see wild life up close and the animals didn't seem bothered by people coming and going.

As he walked up the steps to the monument he was amazed at the sight of the four President heads carved into a mountain of granite. Being so close to something he had seen a dozen times in pictures was a real treat. He stood at the rail and just admired what was before him. He took several pictures and was close enough to get a close-up shot of each of the four Presidents.

Conley walked into the gift shop and asked a young man behind the counter for a brochure. "I'm interested in learning more about the monument."

"Here you go," the young man said as he handed Conley a brochure. "Did you know that each of the eye holes in the rock faces have a giant square stone sticking out of the pupil so that no matter how the sun hits the faces it reflects off the stone and appears as if the Presidents have a gleam in their eye?"

"No, how unique."

"Yes, and originally only President George Washington, President Thomas Jefferson and President Abraham Lincoln were going to be carved. The men in charge of having this mountain carved, the Borglum father and son team, ran out of money so President Theodore Roosevelt pitched in and allotted them enough money to finish their work but then they had to also add President Roosevelt to the monument."

"Sounds like you've done your homework. Thank you so much." Conley walked out of the shop looking at his brochure.

Seeing them in person was so much grander than seeing any photos. Pictures could not convey the magnificence of seeing them first hand. There was warmth in Conley's heart and he felt proud to be an American.

He drove around sightseeing through the mountains. He had to drive through several tunnels and found that each tunnel had one opening facing Mount Rushmore. The trees were cut away so if you were headed the right direction you could see the four Presidents as you departed the tunnel. According to the information in the pamphlet President Roosevelt had the roads designed that way on purpose which must have taken a lot of planning to accomplish. It was really novel and a fact Conley had not previously known.

Conley pulled off the road at every spot he could just to look and take in the magnificent views. One place he stopped was called the Needle's Eye. It was a large narrow granite rock that stood high beside the roadway. The unusual formation had formed a hole in the middle of the rock near the top that looked very much like a needle's eye, thus the name. It seemed to be a popular spot and had many cars pulled off the side of the road just to see it. There were a couple young people using the rock to do some rock climbing and had made it all the way to the top.

As daylight was surrendering to the night Conley went back to his tent. He knew tonight he would sleep sound from all the walking he had done and all he had seen and learned that day. He was hoping that maybe his dreams would take a break tonight and let him get some much needed rest.

In the middle of the night Conley was woken up by something or someone walking in the leaves and pine needles next to his tent.

# CHAPTER 9

The next morning Conley smelled a distinct aroma in the air. He recognized the smell. He saw tiny paw prints in the dirt around his tent. A family of skunks had visited the camping area and most of the people near Conley had left in the middle of the night no doubt because of that. Conley was just glad no one had upset the skunks or the smell would have been much worse.

Conley only had a day or two before he had to head down to the reservation and he wanted to make the most of it. He still had a few stops he wanted to make and some places he still wanted to see before leaving the Black Hills.

He drove into the town of Custer and was amazed to see the modern four lane street going through the center of this very old town with its historic stores and buildings. He wondered how they got the street so wide because he knew they couldn't have moved all the buildings.

First he went into some of the tourist shops to look at the souvenirs. He liked seeing all the knickknacks different areas of the country offered. He remembered in Florida most of the knickknacks were things made of shells. Here, most of the gifts were Indian tomahawks, drums, Indian headbands with feathers and Indian dolls dressed in Indian dance outfits. There was Indian jewelry, rings and bracelets, made of beads and gemstones for the adults.

The little kid in Conley came to light as he looked over each box of rock collections. He had to look over each crystal the store had to offer also.

Conley picked up a shot glass with Custer, South Dakota written on it. He was thinking about getting this for a souvenir when a hairy wolf spider with red beady eyes crawled out of the glass and ran across his hand before jumping off and disappearing.

Conley jumped back and bumped the table behind him, lost his balance and fell to the floor. He had flung the shot glass and it broke against the wall. Everyone was looking. He nervously said he was okay and got up.

He ended up paying for the broken shot glass and a hand carved buffalo about the size of a softball for his souvenir.

He spent several hours going through more museums. He had to know all about how they used to mine for gold in the Black Hills. He learned about how they dug in the mines and used gold pans and sluice boxes to find gold in rivers and creeks.

Conley saw what looked like an old fort. The outside walls were made from medium size logs standing on end with the tree bark still in intact and the tops of these logs came to a sharp point.

At the door was a soldier wearing the military uniform from the days of the Indian Wars. He had on the baggy blue paints and blue shirt. The pants had the white stripe down the outside seam from the waist to the bottom of the leg. His dark blue suit coat had a double row of brass buttons in the front and gold colored braided cords on his shoulders. He wore black boots that came halfway up to his knees. There was a yellow bandana around his neck tied in the front and had a triangle shape in the back. His hat was made like a cowboy hat only it had the gold braided cords used as a hat band and they tied in the front. From his belt the man had a saber hanging at his side. This was the uniform of an officer.

When Conley walked up to the door the man snapped to attention then opened the door. Conley saluted the officer and walked inside.

In the entrance Conley noticed two families all lined up and following a young lady with a simple pink dress that came down to her ankles. The dress had a pattern of tiny white and pink roses. She was wearing a cottage bonnet with a deep brim that almost hid her face. The dress was covered by a simple white pinafore to protect it and Conley noticed that the collar of the dress was made from a hand-stitched lace.

"Anyone else wanting to pan for gold?" she asked.

"I do. And your dress is beautiful. I love the lace. Did you make it?" Conley said.

"Thank you. My aunt made this for me. She is old school when it comes to clothes and does a mean cross-stitch or whatever you call it. She wants to teach me someday how to make clothes like this," the young lady said.

Conley then got in line behind the children and their parents. Conley noticed all the kids were wearing little aprons that covered their clothing. They all followed the guide down a hall and into an area with a small stream of running water across the floor in the back forming a branch.

"Again my name is Kelly. Everyone pick up one of the gold pans from this stack here beside me and find a spot near the creek. Spread out and give yourself room."

The children, four from one family and three from the other family ran and grabbed a gold pan and quickly found a spot near the water. The parents followed suit. Kelly handed a pan to Conley and he walked over to the end. Some of the boys already had their pans in the water splashing and trying to find the gold.

Kelly said, "Hold on just a second. Let me tell you what we're going to do. Take the edge of your pan and dip it into the water and scoop up just a little of the dirt. Next we move the pan around in a circle and let the water spill out over the side. Make sure the pan is tilted toward the water so it won't splash out on you and you end up wearing it home. That's the way. Take your time and think about what you are doing. Once the water's all out of your pan then dip it back into the creek and get more water. What we are doing is washing out all the mud from the pan."

Kelly watched and helped the kids learn the process. The children were excited and talking all at once. The parents were busy helping and when they could they would pan for the gold too.

A girl, about ten years old, with short curly blonde hair sitting in the middle yelled, "I found some! I found gold!"

All the kids ran over to see. The little girl was picking small gold nuggets out of her pan and showing them to everyone. She was very excited and wanted her dad to keep them for her. Kelly gave her a small plastic bottle to keep them in.

The children ran back to their spots and now were really swirling the water in their pans. The gold rush was on. Kids and parents were scooping up more mud and rinsing the mud out with the water. Soon there was another strike and then another. Conley giggled at the parents and the kids as all the children seemed to be chatting away yelling things like "I found gold!" and "I'm rich." Conley heard squeals of excitement.

During the commotion, Conley asked Kelly if it was real gold. She whispered, "No, the nuggets are homemade. The nuggets are made from brass. The brass color has a shiny almost gold color. At one time we use fishing sinkers but they are made from lead so that wasn't good. We took the little lead sinkers and painted them gold. The brass is a heavy metal with no lead and we don't have to paint the brass so that works out better."

Kelly passed out several more of the little bottles. Conley tried his hand at finding gold. When he got the first nugget he was just as excited as the kids. It felt as if the nuggets were real gold.

Conley asked, "Why do the nuggets stay in the pans? It seems like we would wash them over the side with the rest of the dirt."

"That's a very good question," Kelly said. "Gold is heavier than the dirt so when we wash out all the dirt only the gold is left."

The demonstration was a true representation of what panning for gold was really like over a hundred and fifty years ago. Conley handed his gold nuggets to some of the kids that didn't find as much gold as some of the others did.

After the mining part of the museum he went on to the history section. He learned that the town of Custer was first called Stonewall after Stonewall Jackson and later changed to Custer when the military moved into the Black Hills to protect the miners. It was one of the major booming gold mine towns around 1875 until a fresh boom of gold was discovered in Deadwood. The town went from a population of over ten thousand down to about ten people in just a few days.

He learned that years ago when the town was first being built the streets were originally made very wide on purpose so the twenty mule team wagons hauling supplies could turn around when they needed to.

Conley was getting hungry so he walked down the street where he saw a billboard advertising an old west dinner from a covered chuck wagon. There was no building, everything was outside. He stood in line and paid to get onto this buckboard wagon with a bunch of other people and took a short trip down this dirt road to where they served the food.

The place was made to look like an old covered wagon camp with a bunch of Conestoga wagons in a circle and the chuck wagon was in the middle. There were picnic tables around for the people to sit inside the circled wagons. Conley went up and ordered the gold miners special which was a steak that came with soup beans, cornbread and a baked potato and he got the sweetened iced tea to go with it.

When his food was ready Conley got his plate and was looking around for a place to sit. He didn't want to interrupt anyone with a family but didn't want to sit by himself either so he was looking for just the right situation.

A man behind Conley tapped Conley on the shoulder and told Conley to sit with him and his wife. When Conley looked around to say thanks he recognized a buddy he had been in the military with many years ago.

"Well, look who it is," Conley said, excited to see his military friend.

"I thought that was you. You look about the same except you have more hair now and I have less," the man laughed.

"Major Whitman, how have you been? I never expected to see you when I got up this morning," Conley said as they made their way over to a table and sat down. "Are you still in the service?"

"No, I'm Colonel now. I retired a couple years ago and just came out here on vacation. Every year my wife, Marie, and I head out somewhere into the wilderness to camp and we piddle around looking for gold just for fun. What're you doing out here?" the Colonel asked.

"Hi, Marie, I'm pleased to meet you. I'm out here on vacation too. I'm checking out the Black Hills then heading down to the Pine Ridge Reservation to visit a powwow there," he said. Conley didn't want to say the real reason was his dreams though he knew the Colonel knew about one of them Conley had back during the war when it helped save the guard detail he was with from an attack. But maybe the Colonel had forgotten.

Back during the Vietnam War Conley had served under the Colonel, then a Major, with a group of men protecting the command post. One night, several of the men were getting bored and sleepy. They couldn't afford to fall asleep while watching the empty field in front of them. They had a job to do and watching the field for anyone trying to sneak into the command area was very important. Conley had dreamed that when the next moon was a new moon they would be attacked. That night the moon was a new moon.

Conley went around making sure everyone was on their toes. He knew something was about to happen. The others thought he had a sixth sense thing going on, but Conley knew it was his dream.

He could feel the enemy getting closer but nothing was stirring, nothing anyone could see. He didn't know what to do so Conley told Major Whitman about his dream. The Major said he didn't believe in things like that and for Conley to just stay alert and do his job. Conley, knowing he was right about his dream, asked the Major if the men could just fire a few rounds into the empty field to wake everyone up. The Major agreed.

Without telling the others what he was about to do Conley lifted his rifle and took aim at the empty field and fired off several rounds. This made the others jump and come alive. For the next few minutes all the guards started firing their rifles into the field thinking they were being attacked.

The next thing they knew they were hearing people in the empty field firing back. The soldiers had hit several of the enemy with their random firing. People got up and were running away as Conley and the rest kept firing.

The enemy had crawled all night on their bellies and had gotten within about twenty or thirty yards from the compound. It would have been only a few more minutes before they would have attacked and overrun the US base. The enemy had used the darkness of the night as cover. They had moved so slowly that no one had spotted anything. No one had heard a sound or saw any movement of the tall grass in the field in front of them.

As the enemy ran away one of them finally hit one of the many trip wires and that sent a flare off which gave light over the field. Now the US soldiers could see more than forty enemy running or firing weapons. The US soldiers opened up with machine guns and some were throwing hand grenades. The battle continued for about forty-five minutes.

When it was over Conley remembered the smell of sweat and gun powder in the air.

The next day when Conley and the rest of the men searched the field they found they had killed seventeen and found eleven more wounded. Major Whitman only had two soldiers wounded and they were going to live. Afterward the Major had gone over to Conley and said, "If this is how you dream I'd hate to see your nightmares."

Conley's flashback was interrupted when the Colonel spoke, "You're welcome to go with us tomorrow if you want. We're going out with a group to a stream to pan for gold. It should be fun even if we don't get rich."

"Thanks, that does sound like a lot of fun. Would you really mind if I go along?" Conley replied.

"Not in the least. We're staying in the Bunk House Hotel. Meet us there about seven thirty in the morning."

Sometime during the dinner hour five or six cowboys came running out of one of the Conestoga wagons carrying guns and wearing the traditional cowboy boots and hats. A couple of men were wearing leather chaps. The man standing closest to Conley had on black leather boots with silver inlay on the pointed toe and silver spurs on the boots' heal. This was the man that yelled, "We're being attacked! Shoot 'em!"

The rest of the men joined him as they hid behind the wagons and fired shots out toward the woods away from where people were eating.

One of the cowboys was carrying a rather small wooden rifle. He walked over to where a young teenage girl was sitting and handed her the gun. He helped her point the gun toward the woods and told her to shoot the gun and help them save the wagon train.

She pointed the gun and fired. When she did a flag came out of the barrel of the rifle with the word "Bang" on it. The crowd laughed.

A couple of the cowboys acted as if they got shot and fell down dead. When there were only two cowboys left, one started flirting with a lady at one of the tables. The other cowboy pushed the guy away and challenged him to a gun fight over the lady.

They stood apart and wiggled their fingers as they stood waiting to see who would draw first. One went for his gun. The other man drew also. Two shots rang out. Both cowboys were hit and fell to the ground dead.

This performance ended with all the cowboys taking a bow. Conley applauded along with everyone else. The cowboys walked around the crowd saying hello to everyone and shaking hands and collecting tips.

Conley and the Colonel spent well over an hour catching up and discussing what all they had seen and visited around the area.

Conley invited them both to come and see him if they were ever in or around southeastern Indiana. They said they would love to and would try to stay in touch only Conley knew he would be surprised if they did. It is just one of those things people say, being polite. They would probably love to but never get around to doing it.

They all rode the buckboard wagon back to civilization and said their farewells. It had been good running into the Colonel and meeting his wife. Conley was looking forward to their trip and wondering just how much gold they could find tomorrow. There is always that chance of finding the mother lode.

# CHAPTER 10

A shot rings out. A minute later another shot rings out. Conley looks around to see where they are coming from. He isn't sure. The sound had bounced around and it was hard to tell from which nearby hill it had started. A minute later the gentle breeze carries with it the smell of burnt gunpowder.

He starts walking into the breeze looking for any signs of a target or game animal on the ground. He thought it may be a hunter that fired the shots. He walks ahead to the bend in the stream.

He hears a splash in the creek just on the other side of the bend where the creek opens up into a large pool and the water looks deeper than the rest of the water flowing into and out of this pool.

A man in a brown deputy sheriff's uniform is walking over the bank and down to the edge of the water. Conley can't see the deputy sheriff's face from where he stands. The deputy is holding in one of his hands a rather large gold nugget that is shaped like a tiny gold airplane.

Conley asks, "Did you fire that shot?"

The deputy sheriff draws his gun and fires at Conley. Conley slips on a rock near the bank and falls backward into the water. He isn't sure if he is hit or not.

There is a noise on the far side of the bank. Conley sees some movement in the bushes and a man jumps out and is running over to hide behind a large granite boulder. The boulder makes Conley shudder for some reason.

The old yellow school bus carrying Colonel Whitman, Marie, Conley and a dozen or so other gold miners turned off the main road and followed a dirt road through a small thicket of trees into a field. The ride was bouncy, and most of the people were holding onto the seat in front of them to keep from being bounced right out of their seats and into the aisle.

The seats weren't much help in the comfort of the ride. They were thin and covered in a dark green plastic material, probably the original seats that came with the bus. Some seats had green duct tape covering old worn-out places.

As the bus went down a hill and was crossing a small bourn Conley could hear the gears grinding and the engine strain as the driver shifted to a lower gear so the bus could pull up the next incline.

The bus finally stopped and one lady asked, "Where's the river?"

The bus driver said, "Just over the rise thare in front of us. Howdy, I'm Rich and I'm yur gold diggin host today, pun intended. Anyone else from Tennessee? No? Guess I'm the only one then." He opened the door by pulling the lever in front of the dash hard and to the left. "Someone grab this here cooler and I'll carry the container of supplies and ever one just foller me. It's a nice warm sunny day and we're gonna have lots of fun."

Rich was an older retired man. He had a big smile and Conley noticed that he had fun doing this job. He wore cut off blue jeans and a red flannel shirt with no sleeves. He had a round sunburned face with a scruffy beard that had signs of some gray.

Conley waited until everyone exited the bus before he got off. An elderly gentleman and his wife held onto the chrome hand rail and took a few minutes to get down the three high steps that school kids seem to manage even wearing heavy backpacks. Conley was going to carry the cooler but one of the other men had already grabbed it and was almost out of site.

The stream wasn't that big. In places one could step across it without getting their shoes wet and in other places it widened out. It looked only about a foot deep at best.

The group had gathered around the driver for instructions. Rich opened the container and passed out the tin gold pans and a zip lock bag to everyone. The pan was bigger than a pie pan and deeper. Its edges were long and slanted and filled with ridges to catch the gold. The sides were as long as the bottom of the pan was wide.

"Use the baggie to keep yur gold in. Just spread out along this here creek but don't go out of sight though. Try to find a sandy or muddy spot. Gold can be found in deeper pockets or on near sides of turns cause it gets trapped in those there spots. Then just dip the pan in and scoop up some of the dirt in the creek, like this, then use the water in the pan to rinse out the dirt. If thare's any gold in the pan it'll be little shiny gold specks in the bottom or along the ribs in the side of the pan," Rich said as he showed them how to work the pan. He jumped and said, "Oh my god! Look at the size of this here nugget I just found."

The miners stepped close to see. Rich started laughing. "Sorry folks, I was just kidden with ya." Conley heard some of the people laugh and he saw an ear to ear type grin on everyone as they stood around for the rest of the directions.

They watched as Rich set up an umbrella and camp chair then sat down. He looked up and asked, "Whach ya'll still doin here? Go get rich, man. Any questions or problems you all know ware to find me."

Most of the people went to the right and a few headed up the creek to the left. Two men stepped over the creek to pan on that side probably thinking that not many people did that and there would be more gold hidden over there. Conley walked with the Colonel and Marie until they found just the right spot and started panning.

Conley walked on down the creek. He wanted to see where the creek went and what was just out of sight. He found where another creek joined this one and from that point on the water was deeper and wider and the creek had doubled in size. He started panning here.

About a half hour later he saw the Colonel and Marie coming to join him. "Any luck?" the Colonel asked.

Conley showed them he had found a few tiny specks of gold colored sand and asked, "Is this gold? I wasn't sure so I kept it anyway."

The Colonel checked it out and said, "Yes sir. That's what they call flour or sugar gold, not enough to quit your day job but it's a start. You don't mind us coming down here to join you, do you? I told Marie that if anyone could find gold it would be you."

"Don't mind at all, Sir. Why do you think I'll be the lucky one today?"

"Well, you always had that sixth sense thing going on, if I remember correctly. I never understood how you did that," the Colonel said. "Did you get a feel for this spot today?"

Conley knew then that the Colonel did remember at least a few events from their time together in Vietnam. "Sorry, Sir. Nothing comes to mind yet," Conley answered.

"Oh, I found something," Marie exclaimed.

Both the Colonel and Conley looked in her pan. At the bottom were a couple small nuggets about the size of a BB from a BB gun. "You did it, Marie. You found gold," the Colonel said. "She always finds more gold than I do. I think it's a woman thing. Ever notice how women have a way at beating us men especially if it is a manly task?"

"Yes sir, I have noticed that. Good job Marie," Conley said.

"Thank you. Now you guys get to work since we know there's gold to be found," Marie said.

They dipped their pans back into the water and started washing the dirt from the pan in earnest. After a few minutes a lady from up the stream yelled, "Gold! I struck it rich."

Another man yelled back, "How big a nugget did you find?"

"Hugh. It's about the size of a pea."

"Dang it. Marie, that was the spot where we were just at a minute ago," the Colonel said.

Conley said to himself, "No pressure. No pressure," as he continued to pan.

The man across the creek yelled, "I'm rich!"

There was a horse laugh from the chair under the umbrella. "No, I'm Rich. I git to say that ever trip."

Conley heard a few chuckles from along the creek.

An hour or so later Rich yelled into a megaphone, "Ya'll come on back. It's breakfast time."

Rich had built a fire and was now scrambling eggs. He had a coffee pot over the fire and passed out a cold biscuit for all to eat. "We used to serve hot ho-cakes but they were more trouble than they're worth, so these cold biscuits'll have to do," Rich said.

"What's a ho-cake?" someone asked.

"You never heard of a ho-cake? It's biscuit batter cooked on the blade of a garden hoe held over an open fire. Years ago that's how workers used to fix their breakfast when they're working the fields. We tried that here for a while for fun but it was messy and took way too long," Rich said. "Ya'll didn't know this trip would be so edge-ucational, did ja?"

Rich passed out paper plates and plastic spoons then put some scrambled eggs on them for everyone's breakfast. After breakfast people were talking and asking around to see who found the most gold. The lady that found the pea size nugget had found the most.

Rich put out the fire and had everyone help load up everything and head back to the bus. "Our next stop isn't far away. We'll all work together and use what is called a sluice box. I'll show you when we git thare."

It was only a twenty minute ride to another creek that was larger than the one at the first stop. Rich set up his mini-camp then had everyone follow him down to where there was a wooden box-like contraption on the bank.

Conley noticed that Rich was looking at a lone car parked about a hundred yards away. Rich looked all around. After he was sure no one strange was wandering about he then returned his attention back to his miners and the sluice box.

The wood box was about eight feet long and maybe a foot or foot and a half wide. It had side boards about a foot tall. There were short boards in the bottom running crossway down the length of the bottom board. It was standing on the bank and was tilted down into the water. There was an old shovel nearby and a couple old buckets that had seen better days.

"This is a sluice box. It's used to find gold on a larger scale than using the pans. We have to work together and share what we find. I'll show you how it works," Rich said. Then he took the shovel and planted it into the dirt near the creek and dumped the dry dirt into the sluice box. Next he walked over and picked up one of the buckets and went to the creek and filled it with water. The bucket leaked but he didn't seem to mind. He then poured the water in the sluice box at the top end. As the water ran down the box and back into the creek it washed some of the dirt out.

Rich said, "That there's how it's done. We throw dirt in the box and then wash it out. Ya'll will have to stand next to the box and pick the rocks out. Once the water does its thang and gets all the dirt out then we should have gold left in the ribs along the bottom. Take turns using the shovel and buckets 'cause they get tiresome after a while."

The group pitched right in and started to work. The Colonel grabbed the shovel and Conley and another guy grabbed one of the buckets. The rest of the crew stood along the sides ready to pick gravel and find gold.

As soon as the Colonel threw some dirt into the sluice box the buckets were filled with water and carried to the top and poured in. The side crew started throwing out small rocks and sometimes slinging mud on others nearby. No one seemed to be bothered by it.

It was fun working as a team. Conley enjoyed watching the others as every eye was focused on the wood ribs in the bottom of the box. He could see the anticipation in every face and feel the excitement near the surface ready to burst forth at the first sighting of gold.

Then it started. "Here's some! We found some gold," yelled a teenage boy that had come along with his parents. He picked a few gold flakes and a couple small nuggets out and put them into an empty gold pan to save and be divided up later.

There was more dirt, more water and more mudslinging than a politician at an election speech. Some gold was found as they all worked hard trying to get rich. They rotated between using the shovel and buckets and standing at the side of the box picking out the rocks. Whenever someone found a speck of gold everyone stopped just for a second to see how rich they now were.

A couple hours had gone by when Rich hollered for everyone to stop and have lunch. The teenage boy had the honor of carrying the gold pan with all the hard day's work inside since he was the first one to find gold. He asked Rich how much he thought their find was worth. Rich looked at the gold they had collected and said, "Going by what I see here ya'll are making about a dollar an hour so far. But that's okay. We'll do better after we eat a bite."

Rich passed out ham sandwiches and soft drinks or bottles of water from the cooler. The miners ate the food and took a much needed break. One guy even stretched out and fell asleep under the shade of tree.

"Time ta hit it if we're gonna get it," Rich said. "This time walk out into the middle of the creek with the buckets and scoop up mud with the water. Go over to where those large rocks are on the other side. Sometime gold settles in the deeper parts of the creek. Let's see if thare's anything out thare worth findin."

Conley notice that up the creek was a bend in the waterway and a large pool formed that was deeper. The pool was only ten or twelve yards away so he took his bucket and walked out into the water and dug down and got the mud from there. He couldn't go any further or his leaky bucket wouldn't have any water left inside by the time he walked back to the sluice box.

The miners were finding more gold by using Rich's suggestion. The third time Conley dumped his bucket of mud into the sluice box a gun fell out of the bucket and hit the box with a thud. Everyone stopped and looked at the gun mystified.

Conley yelled, "Dibs." He picked the gun up to examine it. The gun was a .25 caliber Beretta. Conley thought it extremely odd that the gun had no rust on it and it looked fairly new. It couldn't have been in the water very long. He checked and found that the gun still had two shells in the clip.

Conley took one of the gold pans not being used and filled it with water and laid the gun in it. He knew it would start rusting as soon as it dried and the water would protect it better until he could take it home and oil it down and clean it.

The miners continued to work until Rich yelled out to stop for a break. This time they had the gold pan's bottom almost covered with tiny speck and little nuggets. Rich passed out bottles of water and soft drinks to everyone along with bags of chips or pretzels. He had some fruit for them to eat also.

"After our break we have one more way to find gold before we have to head back home. Ever one go to the storage container and pull out one of these here thingies," Rich said. He held up a small sheep skin with the wool still on the one side. "We can try this method dating back to ancient times. Just use it more or less like a gold pan. Put the dirt on the wool and use water to rinse it off and the gold sticks to the wool."

"This trip has more to offer than several of the other ones Marie and I've been on. It's fun to try different ways of finding gold. We even went down into a mine once but we have never used a sluice box and I've never even heard of using sheep's wool," the Colonel said.

"I've heard of it once in a story about Hercules and the Golden Fleece. I believe the sheep skin was used for finding gold and became valuable once it was completely covered," Conley replied.

"Ah, yes, I remember that story but had no idea that's how the Golden Fleece became covered with gold. It just never dawned on me," the Colonel answered.

"We only have a little over an hour left to go so fan out and find the big one this time, people," Rich said. "I'll divide up the gold from the sluice box as best I can while ya'll use the wool skins."

The mining crew headed back to the creek to find that one lucky spot, the one spot that would make them rich and turn their fleece into the Golden Fleece.

The teenage boy put his sheep skin down and headed off away from the creek and walked over a hill and out of sight.

The sheep skin did seem to work. There were more gold specks in the wool than they had found before using the gold pans but it was hard to pick the gold specks out to save them.

Conley was standing listening to a song bird he hadn't heard before. He was looking around trying to see where the bird was sitting when he saw the teenage boy come running back and waving his arms yelling, "Hey! Hey!" The boy stopped just before he got to where everyone was fleecing the creek and Conley could tell he was ghost white even through his sunburn.

The boy yelled, "Help! I found a dead body."

# CHAPTER 11

Rich was the first to respond. "What? That isn't funny, kid."
"I'm not joking. There's a dead man over there. I about stepped on him." The teenage boy replied.

At first Conley didn't know what to do or say. He had to observe for a moment what was going on before he could reply. "I think he's serious. Where did you see the body?"

The teenage boy pointed back from the direction he just ran. "That way. Just over that small hill about two hundred yards."

Rich looked around and pointed to the Colonel and Conley and said, "Come with me to check it out. Everyone else stay put."

"What about me? You want me to go and show you where it is?" the teenager asked.

"No, best not. I'll holler if we can't find it," Rich said.

The three men walked in the direction the boy had pointed following the bent weeds in the field caused from the kid running back to the creek. They walked over the hill out of sight from the others. They spread out and slowed their pace and started searching the ground for any signs or clues.

Colonel Whitman stopped and squatted down. He said, "Here he is." The Colonel put two fingers on the man's neck to check for a pulse. "He's dead, alright. Looks like he was shot in the forehead."

Rich and Conley walked over and looked down at the middle aged man lying on his back in the grass. The Colonel said, "I don't think he has been dead very long, maybe a day."

"I bet cha that's his car I saw parked over to the side as we came in. Doggone it, never had this happen on one of my trips. You two stay here and I'll go back to the bus and radio this in." Rich turned and walked quickly back to the others.

Conley looked at the position of the body on the ground. It looked as if the guy had his hands up in surrender and just fell straight back. It looked unnatural to fall like that unless he got shot with his hands in the air.

Conley saw the weeds bent forming a path back in the direction of the creek. He followed the path and not far away found that it came up to the creek at the little pool where he had found the gun. He looked across the creek and saw a giant boulder jutting out over the water.

The Colonel walked up beside Conley and said, "That poor guy was shot cold blooded, like it was an execution. Tell me what you are thinking. I can see your mind working and want in on it this time."

"Well, Sir, I can't put it together yet. I know something is going to happen but it hasn't come to light yet. Let's walk back up the creek and join the others. Nothing else we can do here," Conley said.

"Do you think the gun you found is the murder weapon?" the Colonel asked.

"I would guess it is," Conley replied. "Do me a favor if you get the chance and hide that gun for the time being. We'll turn it over just before we leave. Also keep your eye on the area around that big granite rock over there. I don't know what it is yet but that rock makes me nervous."

As they walked back to the yellow school bus Conley picked a long stem of foxtail grass and put it in the side of his mouth to chew on the end. It felt comforting to him and helped him think.

It wasn't long before an unmarked car came barreling down the dirt road toward them. Conley notice that the car pulled off the road before it got to them and drove past the car that had been parked over to the side. It went slowly past the car then headed directly toward the dead body as if the driver knew where the body was. The car stopped and turned then came over to the school bus.

The deputy sheriff got out wearing the brown uniform and badge and walked over to where the group of miners was standing. "Someone find a dead body?" he asked.

Rich spoke up, "Yep, I'm the one that called ya. We're all panning for gold and this teenage boy here took a walk and ran across the body over thare a little ways. The poor guy is deader than a door nail."

"Anyone see what happened? Anyone hear a shot?" the deputy asked.

The Colonel whispered to Conley, "How did he know the guy was shot? Did Rich tell them when he called it in?"

"Don't know, maybe. This is going down strange. Something is wrong with this picture but I can't get my mind wrapped around it," Conley said.

Conley heard an airplane flying overhead and looked up. It was a small single engine plane circling and when it turned into the sunlight it gave off a golden color.

"Uh oh, a golden airplane, a small golden airplane," Conley said out loud as he started remembering.

"What'd you say?" the deputy asked.

Conley walked away from the others. He was afraid of what was about to happen and didn't want any of the others to get hurt. "Nothing," he replied.

"You said something about a small golden airplane," the deputy said.

"No I didn't," Conley said as he kept walking over to the creek.

"Where do you think you're going? Stop," the deputy hollered as he pulled out his gun.

Conley broke into a run. The gun went off just as Conley slipped on a rock and fell into the edge of the water where he got wet from the waist down. The bullet missed. The deputy ran over to Conley and grabbed him. He jerked Conley up by grabbing his shirt.

"Put your hands behind your back," the deputy said.

Conley did what he was told. The deputy pulled out a pair of handcuffs and cuffed Conley's wrists behind him. The deputy marched Conley to his car and put him inside in the passenger's seat. He held the gun on Conley as he got in and started the car and drove away.

The only thing Conley saw in the car that even made it look like a police car was the police radio. The radio wasn't attached to the car though and was the type that used a power cord plugged into the cigarette lighter.

Once they got to the main road Conley saw two other police cars with lights flashing and sirens blaring coming toward them and heading to where they had just pulled off the dirt road. When the cars passed, Conley could see both cars were gray with orange words on the side that read Highway Patrol.

The two Highway Patrol cars pulled up behind the yellow school bus and stopped. Two officers from each car got out. "Did someone call about a dead body?" one officer asked.

Rich walked up to the officer and said, "Here we go again. Yep, I did."

"Can you show me where it's located?" the officer said.

"Sure, over this a way," Rich said as he and the officer starting walking back to where the body had been found.

Colonel Whitman walked up to one of the officers and asked, "Where are they taking Conley?"

"Good afternoon. I am Officer Howard. I'm the investigating officer in charge of this case. Who is Conley?"

"Conley is the guy the first officer took off in cuffs just a few minutes ago," the Colonel said.

"What officer? What are you talking about?" Officer Howard asked.

"I'm Colonel Whitman. Conley served under me back in Vietnam. The officer, a deputy sheriff, was just here and cuffed Conley and took him off in his unmarked car. You had to have just seen them on the road. They left just minutes before you arrived."

"We're the only ones that were dispatched here. We did pass a white Dodge moments before we turned onto the dirt road. Was that the car?" Officer Howard asked.

"Yes, that's the one."

"Did this Conley do something to be arrested?" Officer Howard asked.

"No, not at all. Not that I could tell. The deputy wasn't very professional and didn't really ask anything about the body or anything," the Colonel replied.

"Okay, let me find out what's going on. I'll call and see if a deputy was called in on this. Right now I need everyone to give a statement to these other two officers here," Officer Howard said. He took out his radio and was talking to a dispatcher back at headquarters.

Colonel Whitman walked over and picked up the gold pan with the gun in it and carried it back over to the officer who was still talking on his radio. When the officer was done talking the Colonel handed him the pan with the gun.

"Conley found this while looking for gold in the wide area of the creek just a little ways from here," The Colonel said.

The officer took the pan and walked over to his car. He opened the trunk and opened a leather case and took out a plastic bag. He lifted the gun out of the gold pan and put it inside the plastic bag and sealed it and laid it in the trunk of his car.

The officer looked at Colonel Whitman and said, "Let's take a walk. Show me where the gun was found."

Colonel Whitman and Officer Howard walked over the embankment and down to the creek. They walked past the small bend in the stream where it widened out into the pool.

"This is where it was found. Conley scooped it up from the middle of this pool while getting dirt for the sluice box we were using," the Colonel said.

The officer took a couple pictures then asked, "Is there anything else you can tell me?"

"Well, Conley told me to keep an eye on that boulder across the creek over there. He didn't say why."

"Okay, let's go check it out," Officer Howard said. They walked down to where the creek was narrow and jumped across and made their way back to where the large boulder was sitting.

The radio called to the officer. He told the dispatcher to wait one second. He motioned for the Colonel to stay where he was then walked away to talk. When he returned he said, "There wasn't a deputy called out to cover the dead body call. I don't know who that was that showed up before we got here. We have a plane searching for that car now and I'll let you know if we find anything."

"Okay, thanks officer," the Colonel said.

They walked over to the large granite rock about the size of a one story building and started climbing around to see what they could find. Once on top the Colonel looked down the other side and said, "Hello." He didn't say hello as a greeting but more like 'Look what I found.'

Officer Howard climbed down the back side of the boulder as fast as he could. He got to the man sitting there with his legs stretched out and leaning his back against the rock. "Are you okay?" the officer asked the guy.

"No, not really. I've been shot in the back," the injured man said.

"We were out here panning part of the day. Why didn't you call out?" the Colonel asked.

"I was afraid. I thought the guy that shot me might be with you," the injured man said.

Officer Howard called for help on his radio. He then called dispatch and asked for medical assistance to be sent to the scene. Soon two more officers came to help. They carried the guy back to the yellow school bus and set him down and started dressing his wound.

"What happened?" the officer asked.

"My buddy, Bob and me were panning yesterday and we found a nice size nugget that was shaped like a small airplane. As we were walking back to our car a deputy came up to us and asked us if we had any luck. Bob showed him the nugget. The deputy said he had to confiscate it. When Bob refused to give the nugget to the deputy the deputy pulled out his gun and shot Bob. I ran. He shot me in the back but I managed to escape. Did you find Bob? Is he okay?"

"I am sorry to tell you this but your friend is dead," the officer told the man.

A very sad look formed on the man's face and tears formed in his eyes.

The first officer and Rich came walking back from the dead body. The first officer said they had called for the coroner and that an ambulance would be here in a few minutes to take the injured man to the hospital.

A police radio crackled. Officer Howard who was first to get to the injured man walked away to talk. When he returned he said, "Our plane spotted the car with Conley. Dispatch sent a Highway Patrol car to intercept them and there is a chase. The white dodge is trying to outrun the patrol car. Your friend, Conley, may have been kidnapped by the killer. That's all I know at this time."

# CHAPTER 12

Conley realized that this deputy was the one he saw in his dream. He had a lot of mixed emotions about what to do. He didn't have all the facts of what had happened. He did feel that whatever was happening wasn't being handled correctly by this deputy sheriff.

Conley really didn't know what he could do. He was in a tough spot. There wasn't a whole lot he could do without getting into more serious trouble. He was sitting, handcuffed, beside a deputy sheriff holding a gun pointed at him while they were going down the road. Conley thought once they were at the police station he could get everything straightened out.

The deputy sheriff was looking in the rear view mirror. Conley glanced back and saw a police car behind them with its red lights flashing and the siren going. He thought at first the other car needed to pass and was going on another call to somewhere. The deputy sheriff sped up. The chase was on.

Conley heard the tires squeal when they went around turns. He saw the nervous look on the face of the deputy sheriff driving. At times the deputy had to hold onto the steering wheel with both hand to make the turns.

"Why did you kidnap me away from my friends?" Conley asked. He was trying to make sure of the situation before taking any actions. He also wanted to distract the driver so he would make a mistake and get caught.

"You know why. You're the one that saw me kill your friend. I thought I wounded you, though," the deputy said.

"That wasn't me. Do I look like the man you wounded?" Conley asked.

"Maybe, but you knew about the golden airplane so you have to be the other guy," the deputy said.

"I was talking about the airplane that flew overhead. When it turned into the sun it gave off a golden color," Conley said.

"Shut the hell up. I'm busy here," the deputy said.

Conley was getting ready. He had a plan to stop this madness and hoped he survived what he was about to do. The road turned to the left and Conley was slung into his door. The deputy had both hands on the steering wheel and still was holding on to the gun. Ahead the road had cliffs on both sides of the road. With the tires squealing Conley leaned his back into his door and braced himself. He pulled his feet up and gave a strong kick to the deputy. One foot hit the deputy in the side and the other foot kicked the gun.

Bang! The gun fired. The bullet hit the seat beside Conley. The deputy lost control of the car and the car went off the road and slammed into the cliff on the driver's side. Conley was thrown forward and ended up on his back down on the floorboard from the sudden stop. His feet were sticking up over his seat. He was upside down.

Conley could see smoke coming into the car from the engine. He could smell oil burning. Steam came into the car from the air vents and he could smell the sweet aroma of anti-freeze so thick it left a foul taste in his mouth and made his eyes water and burn.

Conley looked up at the deputy. The deputy didn't move and was slumped down with his head on the steering wheel and blood running down his forehead.

During the wreck the glove compartment door had been jarred open. On the floor beside Conley was a good size gold nugget in the shape of a small airplane.

The passenger side door opened. Two Highway Patrol officers pulled Conley from the car. They took off the handcuffs and walked him over to the side of the road and sat him down.

"Are you alright?" one patrolman asked.

"I don't know. I feel like I was hit by a truck," Conley replied. Conley checked his arms and legs and found everything was working. His neck was stiff and he could tell his shoulders felt bruised. There was a small knot on his head but otherwise he seemed to be okay.

The other patrolman was checking on the deputy. "He's alive. Call an ambulance."

The two patrolmen couldn't get the driver out of the car. He was lodged into the steering column and the dashboard. Another Highway Patrol car pulled up. A patrolman got out and walked over to Conley. He said, "You're coming with us. We need to get you to the hospital to get checked out while we get a statement from you."

At the hospital Conley was given a clean bill of health. He was handed a few pain tablets for the soreness he was experiencing. After Conley gave the patrolmen his statement he was free to go.

*The old Indian woman is walking her pony down to a stream to get her pony a drink. A storm cloud appears and it starts pouring the rain. Lightning is flashing all around. Conley can hear some type of roar coming from upstream. The Indian lady is standing on the bank when a wall of water rushes down the stream. The water over runs the bank knocking her down. She is carried off with the wall of water. It happens so fast that Conley is in shock and just stands there watching for a second before he has time to realize what is going on.*

It was such a shock that Conley was startled awake. His heart was pounding hard as if he had been there seeing the flash flood. Just before he could open his eyes he heard someone, an older lady's voice yell, "Go!" He wasn't sure where it came from, possibly from a camper near him but he couldn't tell.

Conley did notice his forehead was wet from water dripping through a hole in the top of his tent where the tent pole held up the front part of the tent. Maybe that was the reason why he dreamed what he did.

When he stepped out of his tent it had started to drizzle rain and he knew it was time to pack up his tent and head out to the reservation. He knew his little squirrel friend would be happy to see him move on.

He loaded up his tent and got in the car to leave. Conley saw that the clouds were getting darker and it looked like a very bad storm coming in. There was lightning and then a loud burst of thunder. He listened as the thunder echoed off a canyon wall and then could be heard from the next ridge and then softer as if it was echoing from a distance. It then was loud again from echoing across the way. Each thunder clap echoed many times as the sound was moving around the mountain ranges then returning. Conley had never heard thunder do this and just listened for several minutes before driving on down the road as he headed southeast toward the reservation.

It rained most of the way but the storm was coming up from the south so he wasn't in the direct path of the storm and he was actually moving away from the worst part.

At one of the overlooks Conley stopped the car and looked across the valley. What he saw amazed him. He could see the storm clouds off in the distance in the valley below. He saw the lightning come from the dark clouds to the ground but what he was so taken by was he saw lightning extended not only to the ground about one thousand feet below but also it shot up past the storm cloud thousands of feet high into the air. He had never even heard of lightning doing this. He watched this amazing sight. It was breathtaking to see nature's light show.

Several hours later and after Conley had stopped for something to eat, he stopped at a little store over halfway there to get gas. He asked the man inside what was the best way to go to get to Porcupine, where the powwow was to be held.

The man behind the counter said, "Going down by the Bad Lands is faster but if it were me today, I would take the long way around and drive into Pine Ridge and then on to Porcupine because if it rains too much the Bad Lands can flash flood. Good thing you aren't heading for the Black Hills."

"Why's that?" Conley asked.

"Didn't you hear? Up in the mountains they got as much as nine inches of rain in the past several hours. Many of the campgrounds were flooded out and some of the bridges are washed away. The radio said there were people missing and they had no idea how many yet. I guess it was the worse rain they had up there since they got fifteen inches of rain in six hours that broke one of the lake dams back in the '72 flooding of Rapid City. A good many people died that day. I believe about three hundred if my memory serves me right," the man told him.

Conley said, "Wow, it's a good thing I left from up there when I did then." He thought about the dream he had just before he woke and whispered a great big thank you to the old Indian woman in his mind.

He drove onto the Pine Ridge Reservation and the first thing he saw was the Indian casino. He now knew where to go if he needed any extra cash for his trip. So far Conley thought his money was holding out pretty well.

He drove on through the town of Pine Ridge and was on his way to Wounded Knee. He saw several Native Americans sitting out in a field in lawn chairs in the rain. They had on what looked like big trash bags over them to help keep them dry. It looked to Conley that this was where that family lived. It was probably their land from the Oglala tribe but they didn't have money to build a house so they just lived in the field.

Across the road was a driveway with a teepee at the end of it. A late model car was parked there and the teepee had an electric line running into the smoke hole at the top of the teepee so they had electricity. It was eye-opening to see that teepees were still being used.

It had stopped raining and several miles farther on down the road, Conley came to a place that turned into a divided highway for a short distance. In the middle where the road parted was an old motor home that had broken down many years ago.

Conley slowed down to see what this was about. A man was outside frying breakfast on a grill in the front of the motor home. Conley stopped and asked, "Do you need help?"

"Oh no, I'm fine," the older Native American man said.

"Can I give you a lift somewhere?" Conley asked.

"No thanks. This is where I live. I broke down four years ago and just stayed. Two years ago when they repaved the road they made this into a divided highway so I could live here. They just paved around me and I've been here ever since," the man said.

Conley's mind went blank. He found it hard to find any words to say after what he had just heard. Upon looking around he noticed the man had flowers planted in his yard. Conley saw a weed eater he thought the man used to keep his grass cut. The man even had a beagle tied to a dog house in the side yard. The old pavement was used as the man's patio.

"You have a good day," Conley said as he pulled away.

Conley drove on through to Porcupine. He pulled over at a small corner store to get a snack, use the phone, and ask how to get to the powwow.

He had called Emily a couple times when he was in Rapid City and wanted to call her again and tell her he had arrived at the reservation. His cell phone had no signal here. He asked if the store had a pay phone he could use and he found out the nearest pay phone was seventeen miles away back at a town called Manderson over past Wounded Knee. So, he got directions to the powwow which was only a few miles further down the road by going to the fork ahead and turning to the right.

When he got there he recognized it as the place the old Indian woman in his dream had pointed to. It was nothing like the powwow in Rapid City. Here they just had a large circle roped off in a field at the top of the hill and the people watching had to bring their own chairs or sit on the ground under a shelter for shade.

The shelter was made from long polls and only had pine branches over the top partially blocking some of the sun. There was no charge and no competition dancing. There were only a few tourists. Most of the people here were FBI, full blooded Indians. This was the real thing Conley was looking for.

Conley set up his tent right beside his car out in the field where everyone parked. That seemed to be what some of the others were doing.

He saw that people were getting water from an old hand pump near the dancing circle so he filled a jug he had to keep some water to wash with later on. Some kids were pumping out the water onto the ground and an elder had to scold them. "Hey, don't do that because it makes mud. Go and get a pan and carry the water away from where everyone is walking."

Conley then went around and looked at some of the booths and checked out the handmade stuff such as dream catchers, leather bags with leather fringe hanging down the sides and across the bottom and the handmade jewelry.

Conley picked up a white dream catcher about four inches in diameter asked, "How does this dream catcher work?"

The young Native American man said, "You hang the dream catcher above where you sleep and all the dreams go into the net or web part of the catcher and the bad dreams get caught there. The good dreams find their way down the feather at the bottom and escape the catcher so that you can still have the good dreams."

Conley said, "I'm not sure I believe in that. For it to work don't you have to believe in it first?"

The man said, "The Great Spirit believes in you even if you didn't believe in the Great Spirit."

Conley bought a couple of the dream catchers to give to friends back home and two special looking ones to give to his daughters.

Conley saw a Native American man wearing a single braid down the middle of his back. He was sitting over at a picnic table by himself and Conley went over to sit and talk to the man. The guy was about forty, about Conley's age, and said his name was Chief He-Dog.

Conley remembered that name from the research he did on the Internet and said, "You look really good for your age."

"What do you mean?" the man asked.

"Well, since Chief He-Dog was chief in the early 1930's you look really good for being so old," Conley chuckled.

The man moved and squirmed a bit then said, "You got me. It's just that everyone wants to meet a chief so if you ask around you'll find lots of chiefs here today. You must know your history," then he chuckled. "My name is John Redhawk. It is good to meet someone that's interested in our people and not just here to look at us."

"Now, how do I address your people? Is it best to refer to you as American Indian or Native American or what?" Conley asked.

John replied, "I'm an Indian. I know it's a big deal to be called this or that to be politically correct but I was born an Indian and just because some college professor or government official says it has changed I am still what I have always been, an Indian."

"It's good to meet you too, John. My name's Conley. What's that you have there on the table, John?"

"I make these earrings. They are made from rawhide and have a tiny picture I painted of a woman holding her arms out in prayer. I sell them for twenty dollars," he said.

Conley handed John twenty dollars and took a pair to give to Emily when he got back home. He asked John what he wanted to drink and then went over and bought them both a soft drink. Conley then asked John if he had ever heard of an old lady named Rose Oneshoe.

"Nay, I don't think so but I don't know too many of the older people. I lived away from here much of my life working up in Utah. I'll find out from my mom. She knows about everyone around here. I'll find you later and let you know. Now I'm going to go over and sit with my family and help watch the kids." He got up and shook Conley's hand then walked over and sat under the shelter with a bunch of kids and some other people.

Conley spent the rest of the day watching the powwow and talking to people to see if he could find anyone that knew Rose Oneshoe but had no luck. He thought some people acted like they knew who Rose was but maybe they were afraid to say anything not knowing who Conley was or what he wanted.

Later that evening the announcer told everyone the powwow fed the dancers and the elders only but today they had extra food. The announcer said they would sell a dinner to anyone wishing to eat with them and they were serving Navajo steak. Conley was a fast learner and he thought he had caught the meaning of the Navajo steak.

An elderly couple sitting in front of Conley was deciding whether to go back to Rapid City and eat or stay and have some steak. Conley sensed the gentleman wanted to stay but said nothing in order to keep the peace and go along with whatever his better half wanted to do. Conley wondered if maybe the lady picked up on what the man wanted to do when she decided to get the steak then go back to the city. The man seemed happy to get to eat here with the other people.

Conley just had a way of reading people like this. This skill was usually easy when he just paid attention to what was said and what was going on around him.

Once the dancers and elderly were fed the announcer said it was time for any of the others wanting to eat to come and get in line. Conley made his way to the food line and got behind the older couple he heard moments before.

As they went through the line, each holding a plate, a lady put a piece of fry bread on Conley's plate. The older lady in front of him had a piece of fry bread on her plate and asked for the Navajo steak. So the lady serving the food put another piece of fry bread on her plate. The older lady looking all around then asked again for the Navajo steak and the lady behind the food counter put her hand on her hip and said, "Lady, you have two of them on your plate now!"

This made Conley laugh and soon everyone was laughing even the lady with the two steaks. The food was really good. The day had been most enjoyable and Conley went back to his tent to see if his new dream catchers really worked.

Conley had a hard time going to sleep. He got up and was sitting outside his stuffy tent when a car pulled up beside him and two young Native American boys got out. They walked over to Conley and quietly sat down just looking at him.

# CHAPTER 13

Conley just watched as the boys sat close to him. Conley could smell alcohol. The high school age boys didn't really seem to want anything. Conley thought maybe they just needed company.

"Hi, how are you boys doing tonight?" Conley finally spoke.

The larger of the two boys, wearing jeans and a t-shirt and a red bandana around his head forming a head band said, "We're good, just chillin."

"You been drinking?" Conley asked.

"Yeah, a little. We ran out and now we're broke. It's an Indian custom to give money to someone the first time ya meet them," the boy said.

Conley almost laughed at their line of bull they were spreading. He knew that in most small communities that many people were related so he thought he would see if he could get inside their heads. Conley was going to play along.

"Oh, I see. Just how much money are you going to give me?" Conley asked.

"No, that isn't what I mean. The tourist is the one that gives the money," the young man said.

"But I'm not a tourist. I'm family. I'm your cousin. Don't you remember me?" Conley said playfully.

"No," the young man said. He then sat there looking down and was quiet for several minutes. The boys were glancing back and forth at each other. "But still this is the first time we've met so you could still pay us some money."

"No, this is the second time. I paid you already the first time we met so now it's your turn to pay me," Conley said.

"But I don't remember that time," the young man said.

"I'm going to tell my sister about seeing you tonight and you know who she'll tell, don't you?" Conley said.

"My mom?" the young man asked.

"That would be my guess. You two better get a clear head by morning. You don't want your mom to know what you were up to tonight, do you?" Conley said.

"No, but she already knows. I'll take it easy the rest of the night. Maybe I can sell you something," the young man said.

"What do you have that I would want?" Conley asked.

"We have an old antique license plate worth about a hundred dollars we could sell you for forty dollars. You would get a good deal," the young man said.

The other young man with him then handed Conley an old red license plate. It was a special issue from the Oglala Sioux tribe from 1988.

"Okay, I'll give you twenty dollars for this. But you guys better be careful driving when you leave here and not get in a wreck," Conley said then handed them the money and took the car license plate. Conley made certain the boys couldn't see in his wallet when he opened it and pulled out the twenty.

"May the Great Spirit watch over you and protect you," the young man said.

"Please, just be careful tonight. I don't want my favorite cousins to get hurt in an accident," Conley said.

"Oh, we will. You don't have to worry about us. We're going home now," the other young man said as they stood up and walked back to their car.

The next day had the makings of a hot one. No clouds in the sky and the sun already beating down to where the air felt stuffy for this early in the morning. After being up in the mountains the last few days where it was a lot cooler this heat felt extra hot. Conley had to get used to it even though he liked it hot. He always thought the hotter the better but maybe not after spending several days in the mountains where the temperature got down in the forties at night. The sixty degree difference in just one day's time was hard to adjust to so quickly.

People were arriving and starting to walk on over to the shelter area to make sure they got whatever shade would be available. They were carrying child seats and lawn chairs, had ice coolers and water jugs. Everyone there seemed to know everyone else.

One young Indian couple had a baby looking out from a wooden board that had a cloth pouch where the baby sat inside looking out. This baby carrier was very much like the old time baby carriers seen in many paintings of the old west. They had made it themselves and got many good comments of how cute the baby was and what a fine job they did in making the carrier. The wood board was supposed to be strapped on the back of the person carrying the baby but this couple used it to carry the baby in the front of the man instead of having it on his back so he could attend to the baby's needs more readily.

Conley went up to the only food booth open this early and ordered some scrambled eggs and an ice cold cola. John spotted him and came over and sat down beside him. Conley offered to get him breakfast but John said they had already eaten this morning.

John spoke, "You stayed here last night, I see. I heard it before I saw you over here. People are talking about the guy that stayed all night and was wondering who he was. Today you must come and sit with my family and I'll introduce you around and that way you'll be safe."

"I didn't know I was in any danger," Conley answered.

"It isn't that you are in danger but since no one knows you some older boys may rough you up to get money to buy beer. We're not allowed to have beer on the rez but some do any way."

Conley noticed John had paused and was studying his face. "I know what you mean. I met a couple of those last night. I mean some young men needing beer money, not anyone trying to rough me up," Conley replied.

"Oh, I thought so. Your expressions gave something away. Oh, and I asked my mom about Rose and she knows her. She's my mom's cousin. Mom says she is very old and lives over in the next county near the Rosebud Reservation about half way to where Strong Horse lives. She says I have met her a couple times and I'd just forgotten. Mom sent word you wanted to meet her so maybe she can come to the powwow if she's able."

"Okay, thanks. Strong Horse, isn't he a holy man? I think I've heard of him," Conley said.

"Yes, when Strong Horse was young he did all the prayers at the siege at Wounded Knee back in '73 when a United States Marshall arrested Leonard Knight for murder. Dennis River and Russell Mann staged many protests for the rights of the Oglala people and some of them get out of hand," John said.

"Hey, if your mom's cousin can't come could you take me to see her?" Conley asked.

John was quiet as if in deep thought then said, "Yes, I can take you to see Rose if she doesn't make it here but I'll need gas money. It's almost a forty-five minute trip."

"Okay, that won't be a problem."

John and Conley walked over to the spot at the shelter his family had reserved for the day by putting down blankets for everyone to sit on. He introduced his mom, Ada, and several of the kids playing and running around meeting with some of their school friends.

Conley asked, "How many kids do you have?"

"Eight. One lives in Rapid. She's older but comes to stay with us most of the time to help when I have to work. My wife's here at the powwow but she no longer lives with us."

"What kind of work do you do?" Conley asked.

"Sometimes I work on the roads for the county. It's only a few weeks here and there. I could go to a city and work but then who would take care of the children? It'd be too much for my mom to handle."

Conley watched and listened as John's mom talked to her friends in the Lakota language. He loved the sound of the language as they talked. It was fascinating and Conley was very interested in hearing them speak.

He saw one of John's little girls hiding behind John and peeping out at him. Conley would smile at her and make faces and she would smile back and then hide. After a few minutes the five year old came slowly over and plopped down in Conley's lap.

"April, don't bother Conley. He doesn't want you sitting in his lap," John scolded.

"Oh, that's okay. I don't mind at all," Conley said as he looked at April patting her on the knee and then added, "We're best buddies, aren't we?"

She was looking up with a serious face at John and he looked over at her and nodded his head to let her know it was okay to stay there sitting on Conley. He then looked at Conley with a puzzled look on his face and said, "She doesn't usually take to any people. It's strange that she would even come around to see you."

"I have a way with children. Maybe because they see that inside I'm just a child that never grew up," was Conley's reply. Conley heard chuckles from the nearby listeners.

Conley did have a way with children. Whenever he could he would kneel down when talking to them and be at eye level with them. That seemed to make all the difference in the world to them and they responded to Conley when he did that.

John's mom took a hold of Conley's foot and asked, "Why did you want to meet my cousin Rose?"

Conley was unsure what he should say. He didn't want everyone to think he was crazy but there was only one way to explain it so he just came out with it. "I've had dreams about her that have led me here."

"Ah, I understand. Then you must see her," Ada said as if that sort of thing happened all the time and was common within her family.

A young woman with a child came and sat near one of the blankets John had put on the ground. Conley recognized the woman as being the one he had met in Rapid City at the Native American museum.

Conley trying to be polite said, "Hello, Terri. Let me introduce you to my friends John and . . ."

Everyone broke out laughing very hard. The laughing continued like that was the funniest thing that ever happened. Conley was taken back not knowing what was going on or what he did that was so wrong. Conley saw tears coming to John's eyes he was laughing so hard. Conley didn't know if he should continue the introductions or not. It would be rude not to introduce Terri but with everyone laughing so hard he was unsure of how to handle the situation.

Terri spoke, in-between her giggles, "You don't have to introduce me. This is my dad and grandma. This is my family."

Now Conley joined in laughing but his face was beet red and he didn't know what else to say. He had really put his foot in his mouth trying to fit in and show he had a Native American friend that he had met earlier that week.

All the rest of that day John had a good time telling the story over and over to anyone and everyone that stopped by to visit. John had to tell that Conley had tried to introduce his daughter, Terri, to him and that got a good laugh every time. Conley felt embarrassed over and over that whole day.

Conley spent the rest of the week with John and his family. Conley had felt accepted by the family and he had met many of John's friends. John had told him who was okay and who to avoid.

During the week the heat wave continued. The temperature was over one hundred degrees every day. In the morning Conley sat on one side of his car for shade and in the evening he sat on the other side.

Conley had spent much of the week with April and Joanna, another of John's daughters about a year older than April, by his side. Conley treated them special, buying them candy or chips and soft drinks whenever they took a walk around to check out the booths and just get some exercise walking around and meeting people.

For the moments Conley was with them it reminded him of being with his daughters when they were this age. In a strange way it was like he was getting a second chance at being the father he always tried to be but fell short due to his situation. He knew it wasn't exactly the same so he just took it all in and enjoyed the time he had with April and Joanna.

Conley noticed a group of older ladies sitting next to where John and his family were located. There was one average looking little sweet girl with them about four or five years old just playing and being good. One of the ladies nearby looked at the child and then said softly to another lady, "She isn't very p r e t t y is she?" She spelled out what she didn't want the child to hear.

The little girl looked at the older woman and said, "I may not be very p r e t t y but I am very s m a r t." The little girl actually spelled out the words faster than the older lady did.

The older woman looked away in embarrassment and the little girl looked over and saw Conley looking at her. She smiled and Conley smiled back and gave her the thumbs up sign and winked at her. She smiled again then went back to playing with her baby doll just as if she knew she had gotten the older lady's goat.

The powwow dancing was basically like the powwow in Rapid City with the exception that this powwow had an extra honor dance. This dance was a special dance to honor anyone that had died during the past year. First the speaker would say a prayer and then the departed person's relatives would dance in the ring and the lead dancer would hold up a picture of the departed loved one. At the end of the dance everyone would come into the ring and dance with them or else stand around the edge of the circle and shake everyone's hand as they went by thus giving honor to the family.

After the dance was over the family brought boxes of the departed one's clothes and put them in the middle of the circle and had what they called a give-a-way. The less fortunate would then go and get any clothes they could use until all the clothing was gone.

Near the end of the day on the last day of the powwow Grandma Ada said something to Conley in the Lakota language. Conley looked to John to get some meaning out of what Grandma Ada said.

John replied, "I wasn't allowed to learn Lakota when I grew up. It was against the law. They teach it again now in schools so our language won't be lost. Terri, tell Conley what Grandma just said."

Terri interpreted the words. "Grandma says she talked to Rose. Rose is very weak and couldn't come to the powwow. She said that Rose would see you but first you have to go on a vision quest. I'm to go with you and show you what you're to do. We'll leave in the morning then when we get back my dad'll take you to Rose."

John instructed. "Stay here tonight and I'll bring Terri over at day break and then you can leave."

Conley nodded in agreement.

# CHAPTER 14

Conley was awake before day light and by the time it was dawn he had packed his tent and was walking around the parking area with a garbage bag picking up some of the trash people left. As the sun peeked up from the horizon he saw John's car coming toward him. Conley tied his garbage bag and left it beside the already filled trash can.

Conley walked over to John's car window as Terri opened her door and got out with her daughter. John said, "Terri will guide you with what you're to do. She'll show you the way to Bear Butte, a scared place for vision quests. I trust you to watch over her and this is something of a great honor I'm giving you. I'm good at judging character and I know you are a good man. Terri needs more good people in her life."

Conley said, "She'll be safe with me. You have my word. We'll be back tonight."

"Nay, you'll be gone a few days. A vision quest is something that can take some time to do. Now you must be on your way," John told Conley.

Conley took a cardboard box from John's car that had Terri's and the baby's things in it and put it in his car. Terri and Demi, the baby girl, were already inside and waiting to go. Conley got in and started the car and as he pulled out everyone was waving. When they got to the road he asked which way and Terri said to go north.

Conley asked, "North as in left or right?"

Terri half smiled and shook her head as if to say this is going to be a long trip. "North as in turn left."

Conley had observed Terri during the last week. He found her to be a caring and loving mother to Demi and to the rest of her brothers and sisters. She was a short lady and very cute. She had long black hair she usually wore in a ponytail. She always had Demi's hair done differently each day and it always included small braids forming loops or crisscross patterns making her even prettier.

After a couple hours driving and some small talk Conley asked, "Have you met Rose?"

"Nay, maybe when I was a small child but I don't remember her," she said.

Conley peeked in the back seat and saw that Demi was asleep so he got up the nerve to ask Terri something that had not been brought up and he thought maybe was taboo. "Tell me, where's Demi's dad? You haven't ever said anything about him so I was just wondering. If it's off limits, I understand and apologize."

She looked out the side car window for several minutes. Conley didn't think he was going to get an answer but finally she commented, "Demi's dad was very mean to me. He forced himself on me back while I was babysitting his kids almost four years ago. It was just before I turned sixteen. He kept me locked in the basement for eleven days and raped me over and over. I was not allowed to leave. There was a small hole in the basement door so his kids would bring me food and something to drink when he was gone so they knew what was going on. One day he forgot to take his keys with him when he left and the kids got the keys and unlocked the door and let me out. I ran home. Dad hadn't looked for me because the guy told Dad that I was just staying over to help him with his kids. He's in prison in another state now for something else he did and I hope he rots in there. I hate him."

"I'm so sorry. I had no idea. Did you have him arrested?" Conley asked.

"Nay, I tried to but this is a common thing here on the rez. The rez police wouldn't do anything because he was on the council, and if I tried to push it further I could have ended up dead or something. That is how it works here. The one blessing out of it all was I got Demi," she replied.

It was quiet for the next few minutes. Conley felt bad about what happened to Terri and didn't know what to say. He couldn't understand how some people could be so cruel to other people like that.

After some thought she said, "I did get a call from a television show about it once. Someone called from the Montel Williams Show and wanted me to tell my story on TV. It never came about though because Demi's dad was in prison and refused to talk with them."

"I am sorry that happened to you and, yes, you're right, Demi is a blessing, that's a given. I won't bring it up again," Conley replied. "Terri, I think you are a wonderful person and a great mom. I have watched how you take good care of Demi and the love you show her and all your brothers and sisters. Just a guess but I think you are trying to make yourself a better life and if there's anything I can do to help, I will. I'll do whatever I can, ya know."

"Okay, can we stop and get something to eat? Demi will be getting hungry and I could eat too. But you can't eat. You're fasting," she reminded Conley.

"I am? Well, I need coffee, fasting or not," Conley replied as he looked for the next place to stop.

An hour or so more of driving found them far north of Rapid City. The area was filled with small rolling foot hills that had a few pine trees here and there with one exception. A huge mountain of only one hill jutted high above the smaller hills it was surrounded by. It stuck out like a castle in the English countryside only much higher.

"Pull in here at this state park. We'll set up camp first," Terri instructed. "This is where Black Elk went on vision quests."

"I thought Black Elk had his vision quest at Harney Peak," Conley noted.

"Yes, he went there too. You can go on vision quests more than once, ya know. This mountain is sacred and has been used by many different tribes for a long time as a place to seek visions."

They found a nice spot with some shade and Terri told him to leave the car in the sun and bring the rest of their things to the tent. They had stopped and got a Styrofoam cooler and ice along with some drinks and food to make sandwiches and snacks for Terri and Demi.

It was a hot, late afternoon by the time camp was completed. Conley asked, "What do I do now? Hike up the mountain and sit for a while?"

Terri laughed out loud. Conley liked hearing her laugh. He thought she should laugh more often but knew she had seen her share of trouble in her young life and she was mostly solemn.

She said, "Nay, it doesn't work that way. I was hoping others would be here and you would be allowed to use their sweat lodge but I see they have come and gone already so we'll have to make do."

Conley looked around to see if he could spot what they could use to 'make do'. He spotted the car in the sun and a look of dread came over his face as he pointed to the car that now had those squiggly heat lines coming from it when he looked at it.

Terri cracked a big grin and said, "Exactly! When you're ready you can sit in the car with the windows rolled up until you sweat all your impurities out. You can take one small bottle of water with you. Now, go ahead and get in and get started. Demi and I will take a long walk. Don't get out until we get back and I say it is okay."

"So I just sit in there and sweat?" he asked.

"You can do that but you're supposed to pray," was the reply.

"But I'm not very good at praying."

"Then pray about that." Terri walked over and opened the car door. "Wait one second. I have to do something first."

Terri walked out into a field and started picking some weeds. She returned and folded the weeds into a small bundle and took a lighter and lit the end of the bundle. Once it was burning good she blew out the flame. The bundle was still giving off a lot of smoke as it smoldered. She walked all the way around Conley holding the smoking bundle close to him and fanning the smoke over his entire body and even rubbed some of the smoke in his hair.

"What's this for? Am I being prepared like a side of beef in a smoke house?" Conley asked.

"Nay, this is sage. I almost forgot to do this part. You may have seen it used on the dancers at the powwow before they danced each day. It's used to cleanse your spirit and help protect you. Now get inside and I'll see you after while."

Conley got in. The temperature felt like it was over one hundred degrees to start off. He watched as Terri and Demi walked down the road picking wild flowers and pointing to birds. They walked out of sight hand in hand.

Conley started sweating immediately. After just a few minutes he looked at his bottle of water and it was half empty. He thought he had only taken a sip or two so maybe the water was evaporating. He tried to pray to keep his mind off the smoldering situation he found himself in.

His mind went to examine his dreams. He wondered why he didn't have any dreams this week. Was it the dream catcher at work? He wondered why he had to do this sweating thing and then go on a vision quest before Rose would see him. He wondered what Emily was doing right now back home. He wondered when Terri would get back so he could get out of this makeshift sweat lodge. He noticed his mind was rambling all over the place.

Conley had to settle himself so he could just observe his thoughts much like he did when he dreamed. Relaxing was difficult; it was hard to breath in the little car. He smelled the sage and old dried pine needles and his own body. For a moment, he felt sorry for the next person to rent this car.

He said a prayer for Terri and Demi. He couldn't imagine what they had been through, and he hoped for their protection.

Life could be unfair and he had no power over that. He had to allow life to be what it was and people only had power over themselves at best. Most of the time he was lucky to use his own power and take proper care of himself and what little he was in charge of. Mistakes were how people learn; he'd made enough of his own to realize this.

He closed his eyes but was still awake. He felt like he was going to pass out and that he had been in this car ten or twelve hours. Maybe the sun would set soon and he would be saved.

The car door opened and before he opened his eyes he was hit with a bucket of ice cold water. He heard laughing as it took his breath away. He gasped for air as he went from burning hot to icy cold. It felt good and hurt all at the same time. He climbed out of the car and was sucking in air. He was weak and Terri had to grab him to keep him from staggering backward.

"Why'd you do that?" he asked in surprise.

"Your time was up. You'd been in the car for over three hours. The cold water didn't feel good? Besides I don't want to share a tent with someone that's stinky," she replied still giggling like a school girl at a slumber party.

Conley sat for a few minutes to catch his breath then took the bucket and looked at Terri as if he was asking a question. She pointed to a stream not far from camp. The cool water was now feeling very good. It was the initial shock that set him back and took his breath away. He headed for the stream to wash off.

They spent the rest of the day hiking and talking. Demi seemed to love being outside and exploring and playing. She didn't hide from Conley like she did when they first met. Now she would hold his hand as they walked. And when she got tired she wanted Conley to carry her which he did with great delight.

Later that evening, Conley was preparing a fire. Conley and Demi walked around some of the trees nearby and gathered fallen branches and tree limbs and drug them back to the camp. Demi had helped him carry some sticks he had cut using the seven inch sheath knife he always brought along when he was camping.

Demi seemed excited getting the sticks for the fire they were about to build. Conley had taken to Demi and enjoyed watching her help when she could. He knew she watched him closely as they gathered sticks and he used this knife to cut them into pieces.

Conley noticed she was looking at him as he put his knife back into the sheath on his belt. She had the cutest smile and really worked hard to help.

They roasted hot dogs and marshmallows, except Conley wasn't allowed to eat any. Demi would offer him some of her hot dog by trying to stick it in his mouth as she sat in his lap eating. Conley would act like he was eating it then rub his belly and say, "Yum," making Demi laugh. She would then take a bite and pull up her shirt and rub her belly imitating what Conley just showed her. Conley noticed that Demi was enjoying herself and having fun. She was trying to act big and she helped by throwing the sticks into the fire.

Later that evening they took turns telling stories. Terri had pointed out that no one could tell ghost stories, though, because Demi was too young. Terri told him that the whole family believed in ghosts and that was another reason she didn't want to hear any ghost stories. Conley then just told some nursery rhymes and Disney stories. Conley watched as Demi's big, beautiful eyes got droopy and her head started nodding as sleep started doing its magic.

When it came time to go to bed that night Conley felt in an awkward place. The tent was small and he sure didn't want to sleep in the car or out on the ground. Terri already knew how to handle the situation. When it was time to enter the tent she got in on one side of the tent with Demi in the middle. It was a tight squeeze but Conley got comfortable on the other side of the tent. He dozed off thinking what a great experience he was having and how this was affecting his life. He was like a little kid going on a great adventure.

Conley wondered if he would even have a vision. He already had dreams and wondered how a vision could be more powerful than some of the dreams he had dreamed in the past. What new information could a vision possibly reveal tomorrow?

# CHAPTER 15

B y the time Conley woke the next morning it was almost nine. He must have been worn out to have slept so late. He saw that Terri was gone and Demi was still sleeping with beads of sweat on her forehead. As he crawled out of the tent Demi stirred but remained asleep.

It wasn't long before Terri returned and said, "It's time for you to go on your quest."

"Not yet. I have to clean up and I want to change clothes and look better than I do now," Conley told her. Terri looked at him funny but didn't say anything.

Conley left for the stream to wash and change clothes and when he returned he looked like he was going to a casual dinner party or maybe to apply for a job at a department store. He wasn't in a suit because he didn't bring one but he did look good enough to go out to eat at a nice restaurant.

"Why'd you get dressed up to climb up the mountain?" Terri asked with a puzzled look on her face.

Conley laughed and said, "I have a friend whose life was falling apart. He prayed and prayed as he sat around on the couch in his house wearing only his dirty underwear not even getting dressed during the day because of his depression. The prayers never changed anything. One day his next door neighbor invited him to go to church with him the next Sunday and he accepted.

"That Sunday he got dressed up and went with this neighbor to church. While at church he prayed again. He liked going so he went every week. He started making new friends and his life started changing. The more effort he put into changing his life the more his life changed.

"He learned that if he sat around on the couch in his underwear and looking like a slob God may have heard him but didn't take him seriously. But when he got dressed up and went to church and gave God some respect then his prayers got answered. Makes sense to me so today I did the same."

Terri thought for a minute then said, "Okay, I can see that, I guess. You're ready now?"

"Okay, but I'm a bit lost as to what I'm supposed to do. I just go up the mountain and sit and pray until something happens, right?" he responded.

"Well, kind of. That's the short version. You go to the top and find a place off the main path. Somewhere you won't be bothered by other hikers. It'll be a place that you'll be drawn to. A place that you feel has meaning for you. Once there you'll stay put and not go anywhere else. You just have to observe what's going on and pray as much as you can. Take a couple bottles of water and me and Demi will wait for you here. Don't come back until you have had an experience of a spiritual nature even if it takes several days. You'll know when it happens. Don't worry about us. We're fine. Nothing is up there that will harm you either. Now go," she informed Conley.

"What about rattlesnakes?" he asked.

"Oh good grief. Just observe them if you even see any. Now stop stalling and get."

"What if I have more questions?"

"Then just ask them up there and the Great Spirit will answer them. Geez, I can't go with you and hold your hand, ya know."

"Okay, right, I'm off." With that Conley walked to the path that led up the mountain, looked back and said, "I'll see you in about an hour."

"You're funny." He saw the half grin on Terri's face as she just shook her head and went into the tent to wake Demi.

119

It took two hours to reach the top. The path had worked its way to the back side of the mountain where it was eerily quiet. The silence was so intense that it was like a scream of nothingness. This side of the mountain was in the shade from the sun and it was darker here. There didn't even seem to be any birds in the bushes. The wind wasn't even stirring the leaves in the trees. Conley couldn't look beyond the path he was on because it was overgrown with weeds and small bushes. The only good thing about this side of the mountain was that the temperature was cooler.

He did meet a group of teenagers that passed him heading for the top. It wasn't long before he met them coming back down. Conley thought they were missing the experience of being there when they just ran up the mountain then ran back down not getting to actually see anything or experience their visit. He thought what a wasted trip for them but there was nothing he could do about others so he let it go and allowed them to be who they were.

He knew people had to learn what it was that they were sent to Earth to learn. Everyone had different lessons to learn that would help them in their own life and he was here to learn his own lessons so as long as he stayed aware and paid attention to what was going on around him, he would accomplish that.

From the back side of the mountain the path was steep most of the rest of the way until he was at the top. The path ended onto an overlook made from wood; a platform that extended out from the side of the mountain and from there he could see for miles and miles. It was a beautiful view. He rested and just admired the scene as he caught his breath.

The fields below looked like different colored square patches of land. There was no other mountain this tall in sight. It was a very different view than he saw in the Black Hills where at any overlook he could see enormous mountains and cliffs and valleys in any direction he looked.

There was only one other man on the platform talking to himself. He was asking why his wife left him. He was hurting and seeking answers. It was like he came there to pray and talk to God. He never glanced at Conley but kept talking and asking questions.

After a while he spoke to Conley saying that Conley's people had found the answers to life. He must have thought Conley was a full blood. Conley only stated that he felt this guy would be okay after he took time to heal from his loss. Conley told him he knew this because the man was doing the right thing by praying and by getting away where he could get a better perspective on his situation. Conley told the man that the Great Spirit would look after him and that seemed to give him some hope.

After that Conley looked for a spot off the path to the right of the platform. It looked steep and rocky and not comfortable for sitting any length of time. He walked down the path to the left of the platform and saw a small place where someone had been before and had made a circle out of rocks with a cross in the middle made from wood sticks. He knew this was some sort of medicine wheel only on the ground instead of being made in a hoop that one could carry. The sticks that formed the cross in the rock circle were meant to represent the four directions. There was enough room for him to get stretched out and stay awhile.

He used his experience he had gained from his dreams to relax his thoughts and just observe everything around him. He let any thoughts he had to just be thoughts and then could release them and just be calm. This took some effort but after a while he could release even the effort and just be calm as the thoughts dissipated.

He lost track of time and after a long while, he saw tiny threads coming from a leaf and going to the center of the circle where the two sticks crossed. He tried to focus his attention on what he saw but when he did it went away. He took a sip of water and just sat as still as he possibly could.

After a short while Conley heard a small humming vibration. He listened. It sounded like it was coming from everything around him. It was barely detectable. It was as if the rocks, leaves and sticks were giving off this hum.

As he sat almost in a trance-like state he saw the tiny threads again. This time he just observed them. He saw more tiny threads coming from the center of each rock and leaf, each stick and plant and going to the center of the circle. These tiny smoke-like threads were coming from the middle or center of everything that was there and going to the center of the circle.

The tree had its center. The rock had its center. Any animal or bug around had its center. Conley had his center, a place inside himself where his spirit lived.

His spirit lived or was part of him through this center. This was the place where his spirit joined his body and his mind to make him aware of who he was. It was what made him what he was.

He thought everything had a center like this or else it wouldn't even be here on this Earth. This spirit was what had created him and created everything else around him. This spirit became him and when he joined this spirit or realized himself as this spirit he would be at his center. From this center he could know that there was only one spirit or center for everything that was created. The one spirit took on different forms that were seen as all the different aspects of this Earth.

Conley was wondering if his dreams came from this center instead of forming in his brain. Maybe that was why his dreams could see things about to happen. He thought maybe his dreams were complete and detailed descriptions of what was going to happen and as they passed down through his brain they got distorted.

It felt like he had an awakening. Everything seemed to be all related to each other in this manner. Everything was linked together. If he found his center then he found the center of creation where all things come from and are joined together. Not to say that Conley's center creates all things but more like his center is the connection to all that is created. Things are just different aspects of the one thing, Creation.

First Conley thought everything must be a part of him but soon realized that he was just a part of everything else. He knew that this one spirit forming all had formed him and it lived in his center where he could connect with it all the time. This spirit connected with him even when he wasn't aware of it being there. This was the same spirit that connected with everything all the time to maintain its existence. Everything had the same center.

From now on whenever Conley would see something or meet someone he would know it or they had a center holding the same spirit that was inside him. From now on Conley would see the world through different eyes and have a very different understanding of life and all creation. How could he not? He was very much at peace with the universe.

Conley was wondering if this was all there was to his vision. Nothing magical actually happened except for the smoke-like thread so he wasn't sure if this was the vision or not. Once he had this realization he heard a voice. He almost started to look for where the voice came from but knew if he did he would miss what he was there to see, or in this case hear. The male sounding voice came from nowhere and from everywhere. It seemed to be above him.

The voice said, "Now know the truth." There was a pause. "Everything is one thing." Pause. "The one thing expresses as different things." Pause. "Everything has a center." Pause. "There is only one center." Pause. "We are all related." There was another pause only longer this time. When it spoke again it came not as a voice but more like a profound thought in the back of his mind. "Share this with those who will understand."

Conley sat there for a very long time waiting for more. The voice was gone and so were the tiny threads and humming sound. Only the stone circle with the two sticks crossing in the middle remained. He sat very still taking everything in. This was a life changing moment for him and he would never see the world as he did before.

He never expected anything like this to happen. He actually didn't have any expectations as to what may happen on this quest but what he experienced was a totally mystifying transcendental acknowledgment of the Creator. This gave him an overwhelming and poignant insight that he didn't know existed before now. He wasn't separate from the world any longer. He was just part of the world and the world was part of him. He was changed.

Conley didn't know very many bible verses but a couple that came to mind were his favorite. It was John 1, chapter 1, verses 1-5. "In the beginning was the word, and the word was with God, and the word was God. The same was in the beginning with God. All things were made by him and without him not anything made that was made. In him was life and the life was the light of men. And the light shineth in darkness and the darkness comprehended it not." This seemed to capture what Conley had just experienced.

The longer he sat there the more he knew it was over. This realization answered many of Conley's questions about life but brought up even more new questions that he didn't have before about life. The vision was much like a dream only he was awake through the whole thing. The new profound information was so complicated yet so simple that he felt he should have known this all along.

He walked back to the camp very slowly. He observed everything with new meaning during the walk back down the trail. He even saw a small rattlesnake and just watched it until it made its way across the path in front of him and down into some rocks.

When he got to camp Terri was feeding Demi and he noticed she just looked at him with a frown. He didn't say anything but went over and fixed himself a sandwich and started eating.

After several minutes Terri said, "You were only gone about five or six hours. You chickened out, didn't you?"

He finished his sandwich and went over to the cooler and got a cola then said, "No, I had my vision."

"I'm not supposed to ask what your vision was but if you want to tell me you can, ya know."

Conley could tell Terri was hinting she would like to hear about the vision.

"I saw where everything has a spot where spirit lives in it. You, me, plants, animals. This spot is in everything. Spirit creates everything and this spot is how we are all connected," Conley said.

"What do you mean connected?" Terri asked.

"Let's say that everything is just a drop of water in the ocean. Each of us is a separate drop. No one drop is the ocean by itself but everything is the ocean when it is put together. If water was spirit then everything in the ocean is the same but yet each drop of water is an individual drop. We are all water or spirit and all a part of each other," Conley said.

Terri was looking down and marking on the ground with a stick. "Where is this spot where the spirit lives in us?" she asked.

"I don't know for sure. There's only one spot. Maybe it's the spirit itself that's in us. Like the drop in the ocean maybe it is just being the water and that water is the same water in each drop but we are still a single individual drop. I think that's what I was shown. Everything is spirit and that same spirit has created us all and has formed everything from out of itself. In that way we are all related, in spirit," Conley answered.

"Are you saying I'm just a drip?" Terri asked.

Conley could tell Terri was now teasing him. "Yes, the most precious drip in the ocean."

"Geez, now your ocean is getting deep," she replied. She then threw her stick at Conley and he had to duck his head as the stick went flying past.

"Let's go for a walk," Conley said.

Terri and Demi joined him on the walk. He looked at trees and rocks and birds and even the grass on the ground. He saw things as if he had been blind all his life and this was the first time he was seeing them. Life seemed to have a new meaning. He had a deeper understanding. He thought he had more choices now that he didn't have before and therefore he hoped he could make better decisions.

He stopped and watched as an eagle soared overhead. The eagle circled a few times high in the air. He got down on one knee and pointed at the eagle so Demi could find it just as the eagle folded its wings into its side and dove almost straight down. Conley held his breath as the eagle with amazing speed came closer and closer to the ground. It looked like a feathered missile as it headed for the ground to hit its mark. Conley thought it was going to crash into the ground and die.

Only a few feet from hitting the ground the eagle spread its wings wide to form a bird's version of a parachute. As its wings came out to stop its speed its talons came forward and it hit the ground right on top of a small half grown rabbit.

The eagle hopped to get his balance and clutched the rabbit tightly in its deadly talons. The rabbit didn't move; it had been killed instantly.

The bald eagle held its wings out to get its balance then folded them gracefully. It looked around to make sure it was safe then took flight, holding the rabbit. A huge aerie high up in a tree was its home; the eagle was safe there, and could see before any danger was even close.

It leaned toward the nest, and two baby eagles scrabbled and screeched over their meal. The eagle tore meat bits from the dinner and dropped them down into the babies' waiting beaks.

Conley had never seen anything like that. Conley also watched Demi as she looked on and pointed to the eagle. Conley knew it was one of those precious moments that he would never forget. It was something only seen by most people from viewing a nature show on the television. The scene was so majestic that once he experienced seeing it he would have that imprinted in his memory.

Conley held Terri and Demi's hand as they strolled down the trail. Demi liked swinging her arm back and forth that Conley was holding. Every once in a while she would let go and run over and pick a wild flower and bring it back to give to Terri. This walk with the three of them was very dear to Conley's heart. He was grateful to be there and have them as friends.

He was thinking of what he called a dark hole he knew he had inside himself. He thought of all the ways he tried to fill this hole that couldn't be filled. Maybe this was the center that gave him a connection to all of life and he got a new perspective on the emptiness the hole held. He realized that just being in the here and now was part of the secret. He enjoyed being where he was for the moment and would cherish it forever. For this second in time his dark hole was filled.

Conley had the vision quest out of the way now and the anticipation of seeing Rose soon kept him awake most of the night. He was hoping tomorrow would be the day he could get more of his questions answered. He tried to envision what meeting Rose in person would be like.

# CHAPTER 16

During the ride back to John's house Conley asked, "Why do you live in Rapid City some of the time?"

Terri said, "I live in Porcupine during the school year to help with the kids and work and then live in Rapid some during the summer to just get away and be with friends. I take a few classes there at a community college to learn more about my job and try and advance."

"What kind of work do you do?"

"During the school year I help cook the food in the school cafeteria and also I'm a teacher's helper. I like my job and I make pretty good money doing that."

"Do you go to church?" Conley asked.

"Sometimes I do. I go to a small church over on Eagle Ridge. Now let me ask you something. Do you ever go to the doctors?" Terri asked.

"I never like to go but I do go once in a while. Doctors have patched me back together a couple times when I needed it, I guess. Why?" Conley asked.

"It's time to take Demi in for a check-up is all," Terri said.

"And you feel uneasy about taking her in?"

"Maybe, I know it's no big deal but I have trouble trusting them. I'm always afraid of what they will find out," she said.

"Well, no need in worrying about something twice. Why worry about something before you know if you even have anything to worry over? Just wait and worry when you do have something to worry about. Is there a reason for worry now?" Conley asked.

"Nay, you're right."

"Where do you have to take her to go to the doctor, Pine Ridge?"

"We have a doctor in Porcupine down on Bear Track Road. He's a white man that came here a few years back. He used to live in Boston and he talks funny. People here had a hard time understanding him at first.

"For a long time no one came to his office. After about a year he was going to leave because he only had a few patients. A lot of people liked him though, so they decided to help him out. They told him to burn sage, hold a medicine wheel and shake a healing rattle during his exams and more people would come," Terri said.

"Did that work?" Conley asked.

"Yeah, it actually did. More people trusted him so more people started going to see him. He told one of the elders he was happy now that he could help cure more people. It was funny because many people thought they were helping cure him since they now had him using Indian medicine by burning sage, holding a medicine wheel and shaking a rattle. He was curing us and we were curing him," Terri said.

Conley started laughing.

Terri pointed to a dirt road that led to John's house. The dirt road was almost a mile long and ended on the other side of the long field they passed through to get to the property. It was John's driveway.

John's house was a small wooden one story house with faded white paint. It was run down and had seen better days. There was a light pole near the side porch with a basketball hoop attached. The screen door of the porch was old looking and the screen had a few tears in it.

The yard was well manicured in the front and the side where the car sat was mostly gravel. In the back yard over to one side was an old chicken coop that was now empty. There was a clothesline going from the light pole to the coop and a few clothes hung out to dry. The backyard also had several kids' toys like a big wheel, a sit-n-spin and some bicycles scattered here and there.

On the other side of the driveway was an old shed with no door. Inside Conley could see a bench with some tools and an assortment of other stuff. Just inside the doorway was a nice looking lawn mower and gas can.

In the middle of the backyard was an area with a fire pit with an old iron frame around it with a large kettle sitting on a grate. Around this fire pit there was several old lawn chairs placed in a circle forming a small court yard.

They parked the car and got out and went inside.

Grandma poured Conley a cup of coffee. Conley sat just inside the door where there was a small kitchen table. The house looked crowded and cluttered with a laundry basket in the floor and lots of toys and children's books in the floor. There were crayon marks on the walls and it had been a while since the walls had been painted. Even though the house was a bit messy from all the children's things, it was a clean house.

Conley had stopped in town and bought donuts for everyone for breakfast which was now past lunch time. Terri took them and passed them around for all to eat.

There was one left and April asked if she could have it. Conley said sure so she took the last donut and wrapped it in tin foil and put it in the freezer.

Conley said, "I thought you were going to eat that last donut."

April replied, "I will but I am saving it for my birthday cake."

"Sweet heart, when is your birthday?" Conley asked thinking her birthday must be coming up soon.

"In April, duh, and now I will have a cake for the next one," April answered. Conley thought she sounded proud she had thought of saving the last donut.

This brought tears to Conley's eyes and he picked her up in his arms and hugged her tight as he let tears flow down his cheek for a few minutes. "Bless your little heart," he said. Conley realized that to have a birthday cake was about the only birthday gift for whoever was having the birthday.

"April, you don't have to worry. Next year I will make you a cake for your birthday," Terri said.

Later Conley went outside to where John was working on his car. John had a flat tire and had the wheel off and getting ready to patch the hole.

Conley asked, "Do you want me to call triple A? I have a card."

John looked at him for a moment as if he was puzzled and in disbelief of what Conley just said or maybe it was a look of believing someone is actually crazy. He started laughing and said, "You're definitely from the city. I can't wait for a month until triple A gets here." He continued to laugh. "I can fix it myself."

Conley helped as they used screw drivers to pry the rubber tire off the rim. After much pulling and prying they got it off. John pulled out the nail and used an inner tube patch to plug the hole on the inside. They put the tire back on the rim using the screw drivers again.

Conley now offered, "Want me to run the tire up to the gas station and get air in it? This bicycle pump won't allow the tire to seal."

John now said, "Watch and learn how we poor people do things."

John laid the tire flat on the ground then went over and got the gas can beside the lawn mower. He poured gas over the tire and said, "Now when we smell rubber burning that means the gas has all burned off and the tire is on fire so we'll need to throw dirt on it to put it out."

He then took a match and set the tire ablaze. After a few minutes the smell of burning rubber was in the air and there was a black smoke coming from the tire. John and Conley threw dirt on the tire until it was out. John brushed off the dirt then repeated this technique several more times. The fourth time he lit the tire on fire there was a loud pop. They put out the fire and saw that the tire had sealed itself from all the heat of the fire that had expanded the rubber.

John then used the bike pump to fill the tire with air and they then put the tire back on the car and it was as good as new, well, ready to go anyway.

Grandma Ada, as she liked being called, came around the house from the backyard carrying two tall glasses of iced tea. She seemed very pleased to have company and was fixing something to eat. The house didn't have air conditioning so in the summer she cooked outside in the backyard over the fire pit to keep the heat from making the inside of the house feel like a sweat lodge.

A panel truck with a small trailer behind it pulled up and a guy got out and said, "John, here are all these clothes from the church league in Ohio. Call your friends to come and get whatever they want and can use while I unload. We got almost a ton and a half of clothes this year from the churches."

"Okay, will do. Just pile them over at the side of the driveway in the grass there so people can get to them," John said as he went to get the phone and make calls.

Conley helped unload the truck. The man told Conley he had to come in the back way and they had to get rid of all the clothes as soon as possible.

"Why? Are they secret or something?" Conley asked due to the mysterious way this was sounding.

"Well, you could say that. Any donations like this are supposed to go to the tribal government first to be distributed equally to all the people. But if the tribal chiefs get them first then very little is left to go to anybody else. John and I have been friends for many years so I bring stuff like this to him so I know the people will get to use them," the man answered.

Within minutes people started arriving. Soon there were twenty, maybe thirty, people sorting through the clothes. Anything made of leather such as jackets went first. Conley learned that the leather was used to make pouches and Indian handbags to sell to tourists at a stand over in Wounded Knee.

People were helping each other find what they could use. If one lady saw a dress she knew her friend's family could use she would hand it over to them and they would do the same for someone else. They also took clothes for other people that couldn't get there that day.

It wasn't long before everything was being loaded into the cars and people were leaving after thanking the man for bringing all the donations to them.

An older lady went up to the guy and just nodded her head in thanks. Her son with her asked the man if he could have the wood from the crates. He needed it to do some repair work on his house. The man said sure and he and Conley helped load the wood into the man's truck. Within just a few hours all the clothes and everyone that came there were gone.

Later, as the family was eating hamburgers and fried cabbage out in the back courtyard Conley asked, "Grandma Ada, what was it like when you were a kid? Were the powwows different then? Tell me about when you were a young girl growing up here on the reservation."

She thought for several minutes then said, "The powwows were different. The music was different back then. When I danced my mom made me a white dress made from deer skin. It was so soft and beautiful. The dress is in a window of a store over on the Rosebud Reservation. It isn't for sale, just there to be seen and looked at. It has been a long time since I've been over there but friends of my family keep the dress as a reminder of the old days."

Conley started to ask another question but John held up his hand to stop him and signaled for him to wait.

After a few moments Grandma Ada continued, "When I was a young girl, a teenager, all the kids my age were sent away to a boarding school far away from home. We were made to speak English and I didn't know any English. I was punished whenever I spoke Lakota so I had to learn to speak the white man's tongue. I didn't like it there. I was beaten for not talking English.

"They cut off my long hair clear up to my shoulders. I remember how hard it was to wear their hard shoes. They hurt my feet. I had never worn hard shoes like that. It was hard to walk in them.

"They made me wear dresses that we weren't allowed to get dirty. They thought all Indians were dirty because we didn't take baths in tubs. Before I went there I got clean in the sweat lodges. We used them to purify our bodies and our minds. We were clean from sweating away dirt and we also washed in the rivers. Back then the rivers were clean and we were not dirty.

"We had to study and they taught us about how bad the Indians were. What they said wasn't true. I knew the truth from my father about how the Indians were treated. We took great care of our families. The school taught us lies. When I told them about the truth of what happened and how it really was, they beat me again.

"We had to go and get our own switch from a tree. We were made to go and get the switch that was going to be used on us to whip us with. I used to break the tip of the switch when no one was looking so it wouldn't hurt as bad. One day when they lifted the switch to hit me, I had broken the end too much and it fell off. So that time I was beaten very hard for trying to trick them.

"I prayed to the Great Spirit to help me and when I was caught doing that I was beaten again. They wanted me to pray to a god I had never heard of and I didn't even know this other god.

"There were lots of rules we had to learn. They wanted to teach us how to be proper ladies. They said that the school was our home and showed us how to keep it clean. They taught us how to treat guests. We were to be nice to guests and not start any trouble. When we disagreed with the teachers then the guest rule applied to us so we wouldn't start any trouble but when there was work to be done then that was our home so we had to do all the work. I wasn't sure if we were guests or lived there. It just depended on what they needed us to do at the time. I think mainly they were training us to be servants and they treated us how I've heard slaves were treated.

"Sometimes people came to visit. They rode in fancy buggies and wore fancy clothes. We treated them like guests and catered to their every need. We fixed them food and served them iced tea or lemonade. They were polite but at the same time they talked down to us. I think when they found that we could be made into proper ladies they gave the school money. They took some of the older girls to work for them at their homes. When a girl left the school to go work we never heard from her again."

Grandma Ada stared off into the distance for a few minutes before continuing.

"Once I put war paint on my face and went into the school room and sat down. One girl asked me why I would do something crazy like that. I told her it was to show them that I was Indian, not white. And no matter how hard they beat me they could not change me into something I wasn't. No matter how hard they beat me I was born an Indian and would always be an Indian. That time I was beaten with a stick instead of the leather strap they used for the harder beatings.

"I made one friend of a girl my age. After many moons of being treated this way my friend and me ran away one night. We thought if they found us we would be killed. An Indian man with a horse and wagon gave us a ride back home. I never went back there again.

"About a week later two men from the school came to my father's house looking for me. My father saw them coming and hid me really good. They looked for me but couldn't find me. I was curled up in a wash tub turned upside down out in the backyard. One man even stood on top of the tub once as he was looking but didn't see me. I would peek out and watch them search for me. They looked everywhere. My father told them if they ever came back he would kill them and they never returned after that.

"The rest of my time growing up was a good time. I went to powwows. I was with my friends and my family. Later I found a good man and had my own family. Now my family has a good family and we live here."

It was quiet for a long time after she stopped speaking. Everyone just finished there meal in silence. Terri was first to say something, "Grandma, I've never heard that entire story before, only parts of it, here and there."

"You never asked before, besides that was the past. We have to live today and not in what happened years ago. Today is what is important. That's why I don't talk of it much. The past is just a ghost or a shadow. If you must look into the past find the good things that are there to keep you warm," she voiced.

"Grandma, I am so honored you have shared your story with me. And all I can say is wow. Your story has given me a better understanding of you and how life was. I understand now why my mother doesn't talk about her youth on the reservation. You should write all this down, maybe write a book. It's history others need to know about. I don't know anything else to say. You gave me a lot to think about." Grandma's story helped Conley realize some of the reason his mother didn't like to talk about the past. Conley felt that his mother must have been through similar circumstances.

Grandma stood and asked, "More iced tea?"

"Yes ma'am, thank you," Conley answered.

Terri got up and moved toward the back door and announced, "I'll get it, Grandma. Sit yourself back down."

The children finished eating and were now playing. A couple of kids were taking turns jumping rope while the older kids were shooting a basketball at a hoop on the light pole and the younger ones were throwing a ball then chasing after it trying to get it before the pet dog grabbed it and ran off making the kids run after him.

"John, what happened to the chickens from your chicken coop here?" Conley asked.

"We used to have some but year before last a tornado went through. It didn't hurt the house but it was so close to us that it took all the chickens. They were sucked up in the wind. Come and let me show you my garden."

John and Conley walked over to where John had put out a nice sized garden. He had about a quarter acre of land he had plowed and hoed by hand. John showed Conley the plants that he had growing and Conley could tell John was very proud of his garden as he explained what each row was.

John said, "These eight rows are green beans. I love green beans fixed with a bit of pork fat. I have so many rows 'cause we can dry them and use what we call 'leather britches' during the winter. We call them that 'cause they are a bit tough but have a good flavor."

"We used to have what we called shelly beans during the winter. We called them that because we had to shell them," Conley said.

"Well, now these two rows over here are a type bean we dry then shell and use for soup beans. They're blooming now. And here are my rows of cabbage. See the little cabbage heads already started? In the back there we have just two rows of corn. Corn is cheap here so I wouldn't put any out but Mom wanted some. Now over there's eight tomato plants. That should be enough once they start getting ripe. Some of the plants have little green tomatoes a little smaller than golf balls on them already."

Conley said, "Last winter I found three green tomatoes in the store and grabbed them. At the register the lady wanted me to take them back and get ripe ones. When I told her I wanted the green ones for fried green tomatoes she made a face and said she had never heard of anyone eating tomatoes like that. Have you ever had fried green tomatoes?" Conley asked.

"I tried them once but I don't like them so much."

"What's this here, lettuce?"

"Nay, I didn't put lettuce out this year. Mom wanted collard greens but I put out kale instead. I like kale better so I'll just tell her that this is collard greens. She'll know the difference though. It's hard to pull anything over on Mom. Over there to the right are my hills of potatoes. I still need to put out a few hills of pumpkins. That's about it except for the two rows of glads Mom put out here next to the fence. She loves her flowers. They'll be blooming in about another month."

John pulled a few weeds from around some of the plants as they walked and talked.

As they stood near the garden they felt rain coming down. They looked in the sky only to see two eagles soaring above. There wasn't a cloud anywhere. John looked to see if one of the kids was using the garden hose to spray water in the air in their direction. No one was near the hose. It only rained for a few minutes but John was sure this was a sign.

That night the family was watching a television show called *Touched by an Angel*. The show took place in South Dakota and they were having a drought. The angel lady, Tess made it rain and there were no clouds in the sky. John said, "See, I told you it was a sign of some sort." Conley had to agree. He had seen it rain while the sun was shining but he had never seen it rain without any clouds in the sky then to have a television show about the same thing on the same day and in the same state was very strange indeed.

At one point John put his hand on Conley's shoulder and said, "Tomorrow you'll go to see Rose. Tonight you'll share Terri's room."

"I can use my tent and sleep outside if you want," Conley replied.

John thought a minute then said, "Nay, the dogs will tear the tent down and rip it apart then pee on it or chew it up or both." He started chuckling thinking about what the dogs would do to the tent. "Terri has room for you inside. That's best."

Later that night as everyone got ready to sleep, John pulled out two mattresses of foam and put sheets on them right out in the middle of the living room floor. John said, "This is where me and the kids sleep, that way I can keep an eye on them. Terri will show you where you sleep, back in her room."

Conley notice Terri give her dad a small frown. She then said, "Come on. You can sleep on Demi's mat and her and I will take the bed."

They went into the bed room where Demi was already asleep on the bed. Terri shut the door all the way and said, "I have to shut this door or the kids will be in here to romp as soon as Dad falls asleep. You can have the mat over on the other side of the bed."

"May I ask something? Is your dad trying to fix us up or is it just me thinking this?" Conley half whispered.

"Ya, he has said many good things about you and that I should get to know you better. Dad wants me to find a good man and get married. He thinks you will stay and I think you will go back to your home," was the answer.

Conley was stunned at her remark. He thought Terri was beautiful and he liked her quite a bit but never seriously considered being with her because of the age difference. He mulled this over in his mind. He was a bit shocked to think he was even considered as a possible match for Terri. He knew to have a chance with Terri he would have to stay in her world here in South Dakota. He also knew he couldn't be that far away from his twins. Just being good friends was best and that was what he wanted in the first place.

Conley knew that a friendship is also an endearing relationship. He was hoping now that the friendship wasn't in danger.

# CHAPTER 17

The car pulled up just off the highway and stopped next to an old barn that was slightly leaning to one side and had been painted red at one time. John got out and said, "Here you are."

Conley got out and walked around the car and asked, "Does Rose live in this barn?"

John chuckled. "I thought you'd ask that. She lives seven or eight miles away. This is as close to Rose's house as you can get by car. You'll have to rent a horse here and go by horse back. You can ride can't you?"

"Umm, I think so."

"Ya mean you've never been on a horse?" John asked.

"Yes, a long time ago back when I was younger I used to ride but it's been awhile," Conley said.

"It's like riding a bike. You never forget. Sometimes a bunch of us get together here and dress in our dance outfits and do a mini powwow for tourists. Martin has people come in from the city once in a while that wants to see Indians dance so we put on a little show for them. They give us money and we can make pretty good some nights. We all have a lot of fun."

A door opened at the side of the barn and a stocky man stepped through and waved to John. "Good mornin, John. What're you up to today? How's your mom?"

"She's good, Martin. This is Conley. He wants a horse to ride over to where Rose lives. You got any he can handle without falling off too many times before he gets there? Maybe one that already knows the way?"

"Rose, huh? She hasn't been doing too good lately. She hasn't been down for about two weeks now. I saw her two boys a few days ago though. Said she was a bit under the weather," Martin replied. "Is Conley here a doctor?"

"Nah, he came from Indiana just to talk to Rose. Saw her picture on the Web and wanted to meet her. Do you have anyone that can go with him and show him where she lives? I've got to get back home and take Mom over to the grocery in Nebraska this mornin'," John said.

"Geez, no, can't think of anyone. I would, but later today I've got some people coming from the city to rent some horses to go down into the Bad Lands for a ride. But I can make him a map and he can find it. It is a straight shot from here."

John laughed. "There's nothing that's a straight shot from here. Conley, are you willing to give it a go?"

"I guess so. I won't get lost, will I? And this is from someone that gets lost crossing the street," Conley commented.

Martin said, "Ah, you can do it. We don't have any streets here that will confuse you, besides I draw up good maps. If you don't show back up here in a couple weeks I'll send up a smoke signal." He laughed out loud.

"Okay, let's give it a go then," Conley replied. He knew he sounded like a city boy even though he was from a small farm town. He wasn't unsure of himself except for the uneasy feeling of never being here before. He also had a dream in the back of his mind so he would definitely be on his toes.

They went into the barn and Martin saddled a small brown horse with a reddish mane and handed Conley the bridle straps and they walked back outside. Martin followed and opened a notebook and started drawing something on one of the pages.

"See this square here? That's this barn. You'll ride up this road here about a mile until you come to a sign that says Dillon Pass. From there you'll be able to see the Bad Lands. Go through the pass and hang a right. There's a winding path, just stay on it because off the path are prairie dogs and the horse could stumble or break a leg in one of their holes. Go to the top of the ridge. When you see a crooked tree go in the direction the top of the tree is pointing. From there it's a straight shot to Rose's about five miles further on," Martin instructed as he finished drawing on the paper and then handed the paper to Conley.

Conley looked the paper over and repeated the directions back to Martin to make sure he understood. It seemed simple enough.

John asked, "Do you want me to take your billfold and hold it for you until you get back? It'll be easier to ride without a wallet in your back pocket. Besides if you don't come back I would hate for you to lose everything."

"Can I trust you with my money?" Conley asked.

"Sure, I trust you with my daughter and granddaughter don't I?" John answered.

"Okay, good point," he answered and took his wallet, paid Martin ten dollars, then handed it along with his car keys to John. "Thanks, I guess," he said with a sly grin.

John told Conley, "Just call when you get back this evening and I'll come and pick you up. Now mount up and head out. It's the only way you'll ever get started."

Conley stepped in the stirrup, swung his leg over the horse and sat in the saddle. He waved and headed down the road to find Dillon Pass.

John hollered, "Conley, that's the way we just came from. Turn around and head the other way."

"Oh, right," Conley replied. He looked back and saw John and Martin laughing.

As he rode, Conley wondered if John's trip to the grocery store depended on his wallet. He wasn't too worried because after all they had taken him in and treated him like family. Conley also knew that sometimes family are the ones you have to look out for. He was going to give John some gas money anyway and that is why he let John hold his billfold. He felt like he had been adopted by this family in many ways and he was proud to help in any way he could.

Conley enjoyed the ride more than he thought he would. He could smell the leather from the saddle and the aroma of the horse in the air. He liked the sounds of the horse hooves striking the dirt trail and the snort the horse would give once in a while. He even liked the squeaky sound the leather saddle made as the horse moved. He could feel the strength of the horse as it carried him along. He leaned forward and patted the horse's neck with a couple firm slaps.

Conley made a couple clicking sounds from his mouth and the horse moved forward at a fast walking pace. He rode until he saw the sign then stopped.

Just beyond the pass he could see the Bad Lands open up from rolling hills and fields into what looked like a wonderful upside down mountain. The land went from just a grassy field into this huge depression in the earth. It was beautiful. It looked just like an inverted mountain going down deep into the planet. It had its own mountain ranges only instead of looming high into the sky they plummeted down. It was as vast as a mountain range and stretched out for what looked like many miles.

The Bad Lands didn't have trees or foliage but it had pastel colors with stripes along the canyon walls. There was some green in parts at the bottom so there may be some grass in places.

Conley had been to the Grand Canyon and this was just as unique but completely different. This was like standing at the bottom of the Grand Canyon looking up perhaps. He would love to explore through the Bad Lands with a guide. He was sure he would get lost in a matter of minutes exploring alone what looked like a giant maze.

Conley forgot his camera but knew he would have to come back and maybe even explore some of this unique sight if that was possible. He went through Dillon Pass and then turned right and headed on up the winding trail.

He watched the prairie dogs sticking their heads out of the holes as he continued up to the top of the ridge. They looked like smaller, skinner ground hogs, sort of. The prairie dogs would sit up and watch as he rode by. One of them would make a squealing bark noise and then they all hid back in the holes for a minute. They would soon stick their heads out again as if they didn't want to miss anything.

It looked as if they were playing tag. One prairie dog would chase another and when it caught and grabbed it then he would take off running. The one just tagged would then chase after him or another one until he caught one of his playmates and the game continued.

He did notice one of the prairie dogs standing on a small knoll looking around as if he was the guard while the others played and ran around chasing each other into one hole and out another. Soon another prairie dog would take the guard position and let the one that was watching out go and run and play as if they took turns guarding. The guard stood on its hind legs with its head in the air and watched in all directions for any signs of trouble.

Conley watched as two of the prairie dogs ran up to each other and froze. They had this face off for several minutes. Maybe they were having a staring contest where the first one to blink lost. Conley wondered if the first to move was the winner or loser.

This made him reflect on his own life. Conley lived more on the defense than offense. He mostly reacted to life in the way he lived through his dreams, the way he played cards, and even the way he dealt with women. He wondered if he could get more out of life if he changed and became more of an offensive person; a person that made decisions first instead of reacting to everything.

Conley took a deep breath of the fresh air. This was so nice. Conley felt great just being out in the beautiful country riding like this. Everything was so different than he was used to back home and Conley thought about the great time he was having as he enjoyed the fresh and different smells.

At the top of the ridge he could see the crooked tree off to his left. It was a tree that had almost fallen to the ground but still lived and was just leaning almost sideways. The top of the tree pointed to what looked like a dirt road so Conley rode on following the trail.

After about an hour he saw a small house at the edge of a clearing next to some trees. He saw a spotted pony with a white blaze on its face out in the front yard. This must be the place. It was the only place around. He rode up in the yard and dismounted. He tied the reigns to a post holding up the porch roof and walked up to the door.

He knocked. It was quiet. He knocked again but there was no sound. He looked around the house to see if there was anyone around out back. He shouted out to see if anyone was home. There was no sign of anyone being there. He then looked in the windows to see if anything was moving or anyone was in there. He was at a loss as what to do. So he sat on the porch for a long time just waiting.

Finally he got up and walked around the house again looking toward the trees and down the dirt road for any sign of life. He did see where a wagon had left tracks going away from the house on down the road opposite the direction he had come.

He got back on his horse and followed the tracks for a few miles but saw no sign of anyone. He figured maybe everyone went to visit a friend or relative. Conley didn't want to go too far down the path for fear of getting lost. He would just have to come back again another day so he turned around and headed back to Martin's barn.

When he got back to Dillon Pass a rock flew past his head barely missing him. He stopped the horse and looked around. Another rock flew toward him from behind and this time it hit him on the shoulder.

Conley shouted, "Hey, stop that!"

"We'll stop. Just pay us some money to go through this pass. Today there's a toll charge," was the reply.

"I don't have any money on me," Conley answered as he thought of what his next move should be. Conley was cut off from returning to Rose's house so he was unsure of what to do.

"Wrong answer," the man shouted and Conley saw the man bend over to pick up another rock to put in his hunting sling shot. The sling shot had a metal frame and a brace that went to the wrist and surgical tubing for the rubber part you pulled back to shoot the rock out.

There wasn't any good place to ride to get out and away from this guy. He headed for the pass where the two cliffs were close together. It was the only way to try and escape. He rode as fast as he could and still stay on the horse. The tree branches were hitting his shoulder as he rode.

As he was going through the pass he felt a hard throb to his head and everything went black for a second or two. A second man hiding on the top part of the pass had hit him with a rock from his sling shot.

The second man's sling shot was an old fashion one. It had a wooden handle with the wood going up to a fork or Y and had black inner tube strips for the rubber part that was pulled back with a leather pouch that held the rock.

Conley fell off the horse and two men ran down to where he was on the ground. Conley came to as the men grabbed him and was trying to search him. He tried to put up a fight but was too dizzy to put up much of a struggle. When Conley stood up he managed to grab the arm of the man closest to him. Conley pulled the man's arm and at the same time kicked the man under his arm in the arm pit. The kick sent the man falling backwards to the ground. The bigger man picked up a large stick and hit Conley in the back of the head and Conley fell to the ground unconscious.

He woke up and had a splitting headache. He found it hard to move. He was tied to the leaning tree. His back was to the tree and his hands were tied together behind the tree. His pockets were turned inside out and the horse was gone. No one was around so he wasn't sure what had happened except that he had been hit in the head with a rock and was now tied up. He had no idea how long he had been there but it was getting dark.

At dusk the two men came from behind him wanting to know where his money was hid. "I don't have any money on me. I already told you that. Now how about letting me go?" Conley told them as he watched to see what they were up to next.

One of the men turned to the other, "I thought you said there'd be five or six people riding down to the Bad Lands today. Where are they then?"

"Well, we missed them or they didn't show up. How do I know where they are?" the second man said.

"Are you sure the tourists were even going to ride today? Maybe you got the days mixed up," the first man said.

"It was today. I overheard Martin telling someone he had enough horses for them to use. Next time you figure out how to get us some beer money and we'll see how good you do at this," answered the second man.

"Well, great. This sucks. What are we going to do with this guy then?" asked the first man.

"I'll take care of it. Hand me that club over there."

One of the men swung his big stick and hit Conley in the forehead knocking his head back into the tree knocking him out.

# CHAPTER 18

It was early morning when Conley next opened his eyes. He was confused and disoriented. He saw blood on the front of his shirt. His head hurt and he felt some pain in his arms from still being tied to the tree. He was alone.

As he was trying to wake up he looked at the crooked leaning tree and remembered having the same dream he had before. He searched the base of the tree and saw a large flat rock next to the trunk only a few feet from where he was tied. Using his legs to move to the flat rock he managed to shift closer to the rock. He realized that wouldn't do him much good. He needed his hands to reach the stone so he moved the other way until his hands could feel the rock.

Little by little he moved the rock and there it was. He could feel the ten inch hunting knife with his fingers. With some effort he had the knife in one of his hands and was sawing through the rope that tied him. It took a long time to cut because of the way he had to do it. He could only cut a very small stroke at a time. He ended up dropping the knife once but was lucky enough that the knife didn't fall too far from the tree and Conley could still reach it.

Once he cut through the rope and was free he tried to stand but fell back down. He sat up and had to wait a few minutes to get more feeling back into his arms and legs. He rubbed them and did some stretching until he could finally stand and could walk.

He wanted to get back to Martin's barn only a couple miles away. Conley thought he could make it that far but he was in such disarray he didn't know what direction to go. He even looked toward the sky for any signs of smoke from Martin's fire pit used for fixing food, the smoke signal. He didn't see one.

He checked his head to see how bad he was hurt. He had a rather large bump that was very tender to being touched. Conley had a headache but also pain from the wound, so he was hurting inside and outside his head. His vision was blurred but the bleeding had stopped so he started walking, carrying the bone handled knife with him.

He followed what he thought was the right path. After a while of not seeing anything he had seen the day before he knew he was lost. He walked around small ridges and down slopes. He went up inclines and around corners. He could tell by the color of the land that he was getting deeper into the Bad Lands. He had heard that when people got lost in there it could take weeks sometimes to find them.

He thought he saw something moving ahead of him but his mind was so muddled he couldn't make it out. He walked toward the thing that was moving and saw that he had found the buffalo from his dream.

The buffalo was looking at him as it slowly walked on along the path. He remembered when Rose found the buffalo she motioned to come so Conley followed but he was walking slowly and sometimes shuffling his feet as he went. The buffalo had to stop many times to let Conley catch up with him. Conley worked hard to keep the buffalo in sight. He slipped and fell more than once. The buffalo always stopped and waited until Conley could get up and start walking again.

"Okay big fellow. We can do this. I wouldn't mind though if you wanted me to ride you," Conley said. The buffalo stayed just ahead of Conley so riding wasn't going to happen, not today anyway.

Conley talked to the buffalo like it was an old friend as he followed it. This allowed Conley to be focused and gave him a sense of not being so alone or lost. Conley didn't want to think of the devious situation he was in but was more concerned about finding a solution to his problem.

"Do you know where we're going? I sure hope so. I'm not complaining but we could take the short route instead of this scenic route. That'd be okay with me."

The buffalo seemed to be listening and would even turn its head to look at Conley and snort as if it was trying to agree or at least contribute to the conversation. Conley told the buffalo he appreciate being led through the scenic parts of the Bad Lands but maybe they should just take the fastest way back to civilization if indeed that was where they were headed.

"You know I should've charged that guy at Dillon Pass instead of trying to escape and ride away. I could've taken them both if I had confronted them. What do you think about it? You know I had that dream and should've been better prepared. Maybe it was just meant to happen that way 'cause I dreamed of meeting you too. You are real aren't you? I don't think I am still dreaming am I?"

The buffalo went over to a stream and got a drink then crossed the stream and stopped. Conley made it to the stream and kneeling down got a drink and washed some of the blood from his face. He rested and watched the animal with a head as big as a kitchen stove across the stream eating grass and weeds. This was a sign Conley welcomed. The grass meant they were heading out of the Bad Lands.

"Welp, time for a break, big guy. Hey, do you know any trail walking songs? You know, like camp fire songs only different. Can you sing the one about 'give me a home where the buffalos roam'? No? Okay, know what? I've come to learn that buffalos don't have much of a sense of humor."

Conley had to rest a few minutes. He wasn't sure how long he had been walking. His head hurt to the point where he wasn't sure if he was thinking straight. He looked over to make sure the buffalo was still there. Conley saw two buffalos facing each other. They looked like a mirror image. They stood nose to nose. When one of the large animals looked at Conley they both looked at the same time. They both snorted at the same time. Conley was confused as to which buffalo to follow now. Conley splashed some more cool water on his face and took one more drink.

When he stood up there was only one buffalo and the one buffalo raised its head and looked at Conley then started walking again. Conley followed. The buffalo went over a rise and out of sight. When Conley got to the top of the rise he couldn't see the buffalo any longer and a shot of panic ran through him.

Off in the distance he did see a house and thought it was Rose's house. Conley was coming up through the backyard of the house. He walked around to the front where Rose's pony was still in the front yard. He made it to the porch and sat down again to rest.

He gave out a small grunting moan and a big sigh. The door to the cabin opened and out walked two younger men. Conley recognized them as being the young men with Rose in his dream.

"Are you okay? What has happened to ya?" the taller of the two asked.

"Is this where Rose lives?" Conley asked.

"Yep, how did you get here?" the other one asked.

"I came here yesterday on a horse I got from Martin and on the way back I was jumped and tied up. This morning I found this knife and cut myself free. I didn't know which way to go so I just followed this buffalo and he led me here," Conley replied.

"Ah, yes, that is our tatanka friend, Thunder," the young men said. "Here, let's take a look atcha." The two men helped Conley into the house and checked his wounded head, cleaned it off and used a bandanna to wrap around his head covering the gash.

"You need to go to the hospital and get some stitches, I'm afraid. We'll take you there. That's where Rose is and we were there yesterday to stay with her. We had to come back today to check on her pony and to get a few of her things she wanted," the tall man said.

The other one asked, "Why did you come to see our mom?"

"I had a dream that led me here," Conley returned.

"Ah, okay. She has been expecting you. She knew you were on your way. I'm Little Wolf and this is my brother Gray Bear. You must be Conley," the younger man said.

"Yes, I am, but how'd you know?"

Gray Bear responded, "Our mother dreamed about you. She just knows things like this. I bet she sent us here to meet you and not for the things she said she needed."

Conley knew then that Rose was the old woman he saw in his dreams.

Conley noticed that both men had scars on their chests. He remembered seeing that in one of his dreams. "How did both of you get the same scars on your chests?"

"These are from the Sun Dance," Little Wolf said.

"Sun Dance?" Conley asked.

"Yeah, a Sun Dance is a religious ceremony we have. The scars are from the piercing. We were pierced with wooden pegs that had a heavy string attached that went down and was tied to a buffalo skull. Then we must dance around dragging the skull. It is an all day ceremony of prayer, dance, and song devoted to the Great Spirit," Little Wolf said.

"Come and let's get you to the hospital," Gray Bear said.

They then went out and got their horses and put Conley on the pony with the white blaze on its face and started out. They rode off in the direction Conley followed yesterday leading away from the house and away from the direction he had come when he first visited. They followed the wagon trail up through some woods and over a bluff behind the house. After a long ride they ended up at a little ranch house where Little Wolf lived.

They dismounted, tied the horses to the fence and the two men helped Conley into Little Wolf's car. They drove a long way to Pine Ridge to find the hospital.

The next morning when Conley woke he found himself in a hospital bed. He had three stitches in the back of his head and six small stitches in the front of his head above his forehead. He wanted to get up but he had an IV in his arm so he pushed the button to call for a nurse.

When a Native American lady dressed in white came to the door Conley asked if he could get up and go visit Rose.

The nurse said, "I'm glad you are finally awake. Let me take your blood pressure." She wrote something down on the clip board at the end of the bed.

"Am I okay?" Conley asked.

"Well, you can't get up yet. You have a bad concussion and must remain still. The doctor will be in this afternoon to check on you and you can ask the doctor about getting up and moving around," the nurse said.

Later that evening when the nurse brought Conley something to eat he told her the doctor had not come in yet.

"I know," she said. "The doctor had an emergency and won't be able to see you today but he'll see you first thing in the morning when he makes his rounds."

The next morning the doctor had to wake Conley. After the doctor had looked Conley over Conley asked, "Can I leave today? I at least want to go and visit Rose Oneshoe."

"I am going to keep you another day or two. You're not good enough to leave yet. When you do leave you'll have to come back to my office in about a week to get your stitches checked. Just don't do too much or you'll end up right back in here. As for seeing Rose, you can visit for a few minutes. She's not doing very well. She's in and out of consciousness and may not know you are even there. She's at the end of the hall, the room on the right," the doctor said.

The nurse came in and removed the needle from Conley's arm. Conley sat up and looked around the room for some clothes. "My clothes?" he asked.

The nurse pointed to the closet and walked out of the room with the doctor.

Conley hated wearing the hospital gowns that you had to hold together in the back or risk showing your behind so he grabbed his jeans and t-shirt and put them on. He slipped on the house shoes beside his bed and headed down the hallway.

When he found the room, he stopped. He had to take a deep breath. He was nervous and had to take a minute to allow himself just feel his anxiety. He was excited that he was about to meet a woman he had seen in many of his dreams. He was relieved that he had found her at last.

Now, hopefully, many of his questions about why he dreamed and what they meant would finally be answered. This was the moment he had searched for a good part of his life. He would get the answers that would give him the understanding about his dreams and maybe his life that he was looking for.

Conley took another deep breath. The door to the room wasn't closed all the way. He knocked softly and slowly opened the door and said hello as he poked his head into the room.

He saw Little Wolf sitting in a chair beside the bed as he walked in. "Good mornin. Is it okay if I see Rose? How's your mom doing today?" Conley asked.

Little Wolf stood and said, "Good mornin. Please come on in. Mom is still sleeping but she will be pleased to know you stopped by."

Conley walked over to the side of the bed. He knew at once this was the lady he saw in his dreams. She looked smaller and more fragile than in his dreams as she lay in the big hospital bed covered with a sheet.

Conley was in awe and felt a great deal of respect and reverence toward this woman. He was for the first time seeing the woman in person that had saved his life more than once through his dreams. He imagined this is how a devotee must feel in the presents of a guru.

"May I just sit here quiet beside her for a while?" Conley asked.

"Yes, stay as long as you wish. I'll go down and get some breakfast while you're here to watch over her," Little Wolf said then Little Wolf quietly walked out of the room.

Conley felt strange sitting beside Rose. It felt like they were good friends for many years and had been through so much together, yet they had not met in person.

Conley remembered one of the first dreams he had in which Rose appeared. The dream was one of the first times Conley learned he could trust his dreams.

He was a young boy about ten and this Indian woman was walking with him through a woods. She showed him the way by pointing out different landmarks until they came to this dry creek bed. On the other side was a vicious dog wearing boxing gloves and it was acting like it would beat up Conley. The old Indian woman went over to this dog and rubbed the dog's head. It was a simple dream.

The next day Conley remembered staring at the woods behind his house. It was calling him. He had been in the woods before but didn't remember seeing the place he had dreamed about. Finally he went into the woods and went as far as he had ever gone before. He started seeing some of the landmarks he had dreamed of the night before. He kept going down the same way he did in his dream as if the old Indian lady was with him.

When he came to the dry creek bed he heard a dog barking. The dog sounded mean and he was scared and wanted to run. He spotted the dog and it looked as if it wanted to tear him up. It was very angry.

He got up his courage and went over to the dog. The dog didn't attack. Conley saw that the dog was wearing a collar and a chain that had gotten tangled in some brush.

He very bravely put his hand out to the dog just as the old Indian lady had done. The dog licked his hand and started wagging its tail. Conley untangled the dog's chain and they found their way back out of the woods following the same landmarks that had been pointed out to him.

Once home, Conley's dad called a phone number that was on the dog's collar. A lady drove over to claim the dog. She said the dog had been gone for three days. It was a champion boxer worth a lot of money and she was glad to have him back. She paid Conley a handsome reward for finding her dog.

Conley felt very good for helping the dog find its home. He felt even better about trusting his dream and having good come from them.

Conley's dream flashback was interrupted as Rose rolled over and was kicking the sheet off. Rose was gasping for air.

# CHAPTER 19

Conley ran out the door and yelled toward the nurse's station, "It's Rose. She needs help."

A doctor sitting there came running and Conley went back into the room to see if he could do anything for Rose. Conley held her hand hoping that might calm her down and possibly help in some way. He felt scared and a bit helpless.

Conley backed away to allow the doctor access to Rose. The doctor put an oxygen mask over Rose's face. In a few minutes Rose was breathing easier.

"Is she going to be okay?" Conley asked.

"For now she's resting again," the doctor said. "I'll be back to check on her again in a few minutes." With that the doctor left.

Conley hadn't noticed when Little Wolf had returned and when Little Wolf patted Conley on the shoulder it made him jump. Little Wolf said, "That's about all we can do for her right now."

Conley was holding Rose's hand when she opened her eyes and looked at him. Conley could tell that she instantly recognized him from the sparkle in her eyes. Conley looked at her gray hair and her high cheek bones. Then he looked back into her sunken dark eyes.

She took the oxygen mask off and said in a very soft and weak voice, "I knew you were here. I knew you would make it."

"It's so good to meet you," Conley said.

"Oh, come on. We've been friends a long time now. You have questions and I needed you here to understand," Rose said.

"Yes, I'm here," Conley said.

"Good. I've fought hard to stay until you came to see me. Could you get me some water?"

Conley looked over at the tray beside the bed and picked up a glass of ice water that had a straw. He held it down and Rose took a few sips.

"I have a lot of trouble figuring out my dreams and was hoping you could help. But now that I'm here I don't know what to ask. Once you're better we'll talk because I do have some things I want to know."

"I reckon you do. Not knowing our ways makes it harder for you. Now that you see how we live and understand our ways a bit better it will be easier. But for now I must rest. We'll talk later. I promise." Rose closed her eyes and drifted back asleep.

"She will too, you know," Little Wolf said.

"She will what?" Conley asked.

"She will keep that promise. I don't remember a time when Mom made a promise she didn't keep. That is just the kind of woman she is," Little Wolf said he then went over and sat in one of the chairs next to Rose's bed.

As Conley stood there still holding Rose's hand he thought about the dream and events that happened at Dillon Pass. If he had figured out how to get away from the guys who tried to rob him he may not have ever met Rose. Maybe that is why his dream didn't have an answer on how to deal with those two robbers. Sometimes things happen the way they are supposed to work out.

Conley sat with Little Wolf most of that day. Rose slept and Conley could only wait to talk with her. Conley looked forward to the next morning. Hopefully Rose would be better.

The next morning when the doctor came into see Conley he was already awake. Conley was in good spirits.

The doctor said, "Tomorrow you can go if your vitals are good."

"That's okay Doc. I'll just visit with Rose again today," Conley said.

"I am afraid that won't be possible."

"What do you mean?"

"Rose crossed over last night," the doctor told Conley.

"Crossed over? You mean she died?"

"I am afraid so. She went into a coma late yesterday evening and we lost her last night."

Conley was in shock. How would he be able to help his daughters now? Why did this have to happen when it did, especially since he was so close to finding the answers he came all this way to find?

Just moments ago Conley was so happy and was so eager to go visit Rose again. Now he was very much saddened and depressed. He wanted to just go back to bed and stay there the rest of the day.


The next evening Conley was dismissed and was leaving the hospital. He was very sad at not getting to talk with Rose about the dreams before she passed away. He had traveled so far and was so close to finding the answers. Conley had lost a good friend, a lifelong friend he had just met.

He was wondering now if his trip had come to an end. He knew that Rose was the old woman in his dream but he would probably never know if he was related to Rose. He wondered if now the dreams with Rose would be gone also.

He walked outside and saw John leaning against the Geo rental car and waved. John said, "The hospital isn't one of our most visited tourist attractions but I see you're trying to take everything in while you're here."

Conley smiled because he was glad to see John and said, "I guess. My head got a flat in it and I had to get someone to take it off the rim and sew it back together. I see Grandma in the car. Are we going somewhere?" He waved to Grandma Ada.

"Yep, get in. We have to stop by Wounded Knee on the way home. Here is your wallet." John threw Conley the billfold as

Conley got in the back seat. "I had to use a twenty because I didn't have enough money to get all the groceries the other day."

"Ah, so you are an honest thief. At least you tell me after you take the money," Conley ribbed.

John squirmed a bit then said, "I'm no crook. I will pay you back."

"No you won't. I don't want it back. I am glad I can help out. Besides, I said I would give you gas money. I was just teasing you to watch you wiggle," Conley smiled. He saw that John didn't like the comment so Conley patted John on the shoulder and said, "No, it's really okay. I didn't mean any harm. If you hadn't asked to keep the wallet it would all be gone so I am grateful."

"The horse you got from Martin came back to the barn. The next day he called and we went looking for you. We rode up to Rose's house and no one was home so we looked around then came home. We thought we would at least find you along the trail. Later we heard from Little Wolf what had happened."

"Thanks, I was out chasing a buffalo," Conley grinned. "I kind of got lost then ended up with some nurses taking care of me."

Grandma Ada then said, "I was a nurse here for many years."

John said, "Last week Mom couldn't walk very well. She had an ingrown toe nail. We tried and tried to get her to come to the hospital but she refused. Finally it hurt so bad she said she would go but not until she packed up everything she owned in boxes."

"Grandma, are you okay? Why didn't you want to go to the hospital if you used to work in one?" Conley asked.

"Ya, I'm good now. I had to pack all my stuff before I went to the hospital so if I died my stuff would be ready to give away at the next powwow. People go to the hospital to die," she said.

"But they also go to get better, don't they?" Conley asked a bit confused.

"Ya, sometimes they do. I had to make sure I was ready, is all."

John said, "It is just our custom. Once she went everything was okay and she is much better now."

"I didn't know you had worked in a hospital. No wonder everyone treated me so well," Conley smiled.

When they got to Wounded Knee John turned left and went past the memorial cemetery that was up on a hill. There was a burned-out church foundation at the far end. Conley could see the chain link fence around the cemetery with the wrought iron gate that was open. There were a few people there and Conley could see many red leather or cloth pouches of tobacco tied to the fence above some of the graves which customarily was used to serve as prayers.

Across the road were a couple stands with Native Americans selling their crafts. Conley could see dream catchers hanging from a line across the front and small pouches sitting on the tables.

Beside the tables was a small teepee set up for people to look inside. There was a red blanket on the ground next to the teepee with some large leather bags and a few paintings for sell leaning up against the teepee.

John headed on through the small town and to the other side where there were many cars parked along the side of the road at another cemetery. He parked and everyone got out.

They walked up the hill to where a large group of people were standing next to a freshly dug grave. A minister was finishing up a prayer then another man, a holy man, did some kind of ceremony for the departed as he burned sage and waved an eagle feather and chanted.

Conley looked around and saw Little Wolf and Gray Bear and then knew the dearly departed was Rose. There were a great many people standing around and some he recognized from the powwow. Conley knew that Rose must have had many friends.

After the ceremony, as some people were leaving, Conley went over to Little Wolf and Gray Bear and told them how sorry he was for their loss. He told them thanks for helping him get to the hospital the other day.

Gray Bear nodded and walked away to meet others and shake some hands and tell them thanks for coming. Little Wolf handed Conley a brown paper bag and said, "Mother made this for you. She said she wanted you to have it and said that you would know what it was about and how to use it."

"Thank you so much," Conley said as he opened the bag and looked inside. It was a blue dream catcher with light blue webbing and an eagle feather hanging down from the center. "This is very special to me. I just barely got to meet her."

"Ah, but you did meet her before though, didn't you? Now I must go. We have no word for good-bye in our language. We believe that once our paths have crossed that we will meet again either in this life or the next one."

Conley thought what a wonderful belief this was. It was not so different from the Christian teachings. Conley thought we so casually say good-bye which now seemed to mean good-bye forever once he thought about it. Maybe that was why he always said 'see you later' when someone left.

"I left the knife I found on the table in your house," Conley said.

"Ya, I saw it there. It was a knife I lost many years ago," he replied.

"Ah, good deal. Now you have it back." Conley then asked Little Wolf, "Do you know if Rose was related to me through any ancestors? Did she ever talk about anything along these lines?"

Little Wolf answered, "Nay, I'm not sure. If she did, it was when I was much younger and I didn't listen. Back as a child I didn't have any interest in this sort of thing. Besides, it is not so important. We're all family."

"We are all family, aren't we? That's what I learned on my vision quest," Conley repeated.

"See you later," Little Wolf said as he smiled and walked away to greet some of the other people as they were leaving to go to their cars.

"It's good to see you again," a man said to Conley.

Conley turned and saw it was Longknife.

"Good to see you again too, my friend," Conley said.

"I'm sorry I did not tell you I knew Rose when you asked back in Rapid. I didn't know the name of my dreamwalker until the day before she died. That was when she came to me in a dream and revealed her name to me. I hope you don't have bad feeling towards me for this," Longknife said.

"No, not at all. I understand. Rose came to you in dreams too?" Conley asked.

"Yes, she was my dreamwalker. She guided me through many of my dreams."

"Dreamwalker?" Conley asked.

"Yes, a dreamwalker is one that uses dreams to help or heal others. She's the reason I found that job in Chicago. She guides me by coming into my dreams and letting me know what to do," Longknife said.

"Is a dreamwalker the same as a dream guide?"

"Kinda the same. A dream guide mostly just explains dreams while a dreamwalker comes into your dreams to help on a more personal level."

"So, you only met her in dreams too, I'm guessing?" Conley asked.

"Maybe I met her once a very long time ago. She started coming into my dreams several years back. I'd done research of my ancestors while I was taking some classes at the college. I was studying art and painting and needed to fill in a few other subjects. Once I found out I was related to Chief Crazy Horse is when my dreams with her as my dreamwalker started," Longknife said.

"I just found out that I was related to Chief Crazy Horse not long before I made this trip. I have seen this Indian woman in dreams guiding me since I was a child. A friend said that this lady may be my dream guide so I came out here to find out," Conley said.

"It's like we are dream bothers or dream cousins, at the very least," Longknife said.

"Yes, and we now have to stay in touch," Conley said. He then gave Longknife his address and phone number and took Longknife's information.

After the farewells, Conley was walking back to the car wondering if this was one of the reasons Rose wanted him to come to find her, to meet another person she dream-walked with.

Was this what she meant when she said she would talk with him again soon? She had promised.

Conley felt sad about Rose dying and now glad that he found another person that dreamed like he did. He felt somewhat comforted by some of the answers he had found. He still needed to understand the dreams to help with his twin daughters and their dreams if he could. He did feel just a step or two closer to answers and now there was another person he could at least talk to about the dreams.

When they got back to John's house Conley got out on John's side and ran around to help Grandma Ada get out of the car. He ran into the house to see Terri. The kids were all watching television with their aunt but Terri and Demi were not there. He went to the back bedroom and looked for them. They were gone. When he walked slowly back to the living room Grandma Ada said, "Terri and Demi left to go back to Rapid City yesterday."

"Oh, okay," Conley was disappointed. He was quiet for a long time just pretending to watch the television show the kids were enjoying.

"I need to change my clothes," Grandma Ada said after several minutes.

Conley looked at her. She was wearing a plain but clean dress and had her hair fixed. He knew this was probably her Sunday best that she wore to the funeral. He said, "Grandma, you look very good all dressed up."

She smiled and when she stood up she straightened out her dress and walked back to her bedroom to change. Conley thought she seemed pleased someone had noticed and he was glad he thought to say something.

He often forgot things like this and was working to change this in his life. He had a love for others but knew they had no idea unless he spoke up especially at times like this. He was trying to be more aware of how others felt.

For the first time he realized being so wrapped up in his dream world had left a void in his dealings with other people. He knew his dreams helped others but at the same time others had no idea how Conley felt about them since he just did what he needed to do in order to help, then moved on. He had always figured the deed showed how he felt and was now realizing that wasn't always the case. Conley knew he wanted to change this and let other into his world and that would take some practice.

John came over and sat in the floor with the kids next to where Conley was sitting on the couch. April came over and sat next to Conley and held his hand. He put his arm around April and gave her a squeeze. She giggled.

Conley was thinking of taking a walk outside when John spoke, "You are a family man at heart. You're much like me. You need a family to complete who you are."

"When did you become so wise, John Redhawk?" Conley said before thinking.

"I can see it in everything you do, in the things you don't say," was the reply.

"Like what, for instance?" Conley asked.

"Like you don't talk of partying or of all the wild women you know. It is things like that you don't speak of that lets me know who you really are," John replied.

"I don't deny it but it may not be meant to happen. John, do you think moms know when their sons won't do well in relationships?" Conley asked. "I was always taught how to cook and clean and take care of myself. Sometimes that makes me think moms know in advance how we will turn out. Men that never had to learn how to do all those things never seem to have any difficulty finding someone to do that for them."

"I don't know. You just don't push hard enough to see if it is meant to happen or not. That's your problem. Here's Terri's phone number," and John handed Conley a piece of paper with a phone number on it.

"Did Terri want me to call? Did she say anything about me before she left?" Conley asked.

"No, but she also says much in her silence."

Conley rose and was going to the door to take a walk and get some fresh air. April got up to go with Conley and John took her hand and made her sit back down.

Conley took a long walk up the lane to think. He sure had a lot on his mind from the last few days.

He walked out into a field. He gathered a big handful of sage and put it in the bag with his dream catcher. What John had said was bothering him. He knew it was the truth.

He knew he missed having a family. He tried to be as close as he could to his twin daughters even though they were raised in another state by their mom. He had missed out on so much as they grew up. He did see them often but it wasn't the same as having them with him every day.

He always knew the empty hole inside him needed to be filled with a family. He wished things would have worked out differently with his girls and their mom but that didn't happen. They remained friends and he did share in their lives but he still felt left out.

After supper that evening Conley told John he had to go back to Rapid City in the morning. He told John he didn't know if he would return or not.

"I know," John said. "I would do the same. We never know what tomorrow will bring us so we have to look at where we are today. Only by seeing where we are now can we know what direction we must try and walk tomorrow."

# CHAPTER 20

*An old Indian lady is standing beside a spotted pony with a blaze on its forehead. She is making a blue dream catcher with light blue webbing. When she is done she takes an eagle feather from her hair and puts it on the dream catcher at the bottom and then puts the dream catcher in a brown paper bag.*

*Conley then sees two little girls dressed very much alike about a year apart in age. They are playing together. He watches them as they grow up right before his eyes. One of the little girls is Rose. The other little girl Conley recognizes as his grandmother, Violet. They are sisters.*

*For a second Conley sees another little girl staring at a tiger chasing a ping pong ball until the tiger pounces on it and crushes it.*

*Next Conley spots a man hiding in the bushes. This man has a scar on his left cheek. He comes out and is running after a Native American lady. When he catches her and turns her around Conley can see the lady is Terri. The man picks her up and swings her by holding her around the waist. He hears Demi cry out from somewhere.*

*Conley tries to see where this was happening. All he can see around them is a giant stone horse sitting on a mountain off in the distance.*

He woke with a jerk. He opened his eyes. Conley saw where a dream catcher had fallen from the head board of the bed and hit his face. He thought that was why he dreamed of the blue dream catcher and maybe he had dreamed of the two little girls because of April and Demi. He was wondering if he dreamed of Rose because the dream catcher fell or if she could still visit his dreams. He wasn't sure. He was thinking about the rest of the dream. It hadn't happened yet so he knew to look for clues pertaining to that part of the dream. He felt he had to be near Terri and protect her.

He got out of bed and very quietly walked into the kitchen. As he passed the sleeping family on the floor in the living room he heard a little girl cry again. It was April. She turned over, sighed and continued to sleep.

Conley didn't want to have a big ordeal made about him leaving. He also knew Grandma Ada wouldn't accept any money from him for all his time he spent with them. He left fifty dollars under Grandma Ada's coffee cup where only she would find it later that morning. He then took a red crayon and colored in a red heart on a piece of paper and put April's name on it. He took it in and left it beside where she was sleeping. He then went outside and got in the Geo rented car and left for Rapid City.

The first thing Conley did when he got back to Rapid City was to call Terri. She didn't answer and the call went to voice mail. The voice mail said it was full so he couldn't leave a message. That could only mean one of two things. Either Terri couldn't figure out how to use voice mail which Conley doubted very much or she was avoiding unknown calls due to some kind of trouble.

Conley then sent a text that read, "Its Conley." He waited a few minutes to see if she would call back and when she didn't he called her again. This time she answered with a hello.

"Hey, what are you up to?" Conley asked. He could hear Demi fussing in the back ground so he added, "Anything the matter? I hear Demi."

"Ya, she's hungry so I was going to the store to get some food."

"Ah, okay. I'm over here at Cousin Larry's Diner. Come on over and I will buy us lunch," Conley suggested.

"Umm, I don't know. I'll come meet you there and maybe we can go somewhere else, if that's alright with you."

"Sure, see you when you get here," and with that Conley hung up.

Around thirty minutes later, Terri and Demi walked up to the rented Geo and opened the door and got in.

"Hi, I didn't see you pull in. Why don't you want to eat here? Isn't the food any good?" Conley asked.

"I don't know. I've never eaten here but there are certain places Indian's don't go when they are off the rez and this is one of them," Terri answered. "That's why I parked across the street."

"I don't understand. What's the problem? Can you explain to me what you are talking about?" Conley asked.

"Sure, that's easy. I'll show you," she said as she opened the car door and she and Demi got back out. "Come on and let's go in."

As the three of them walked into the restaurant she said, "Just promise me not to start any trouble because I'm the one that will go to jail. That's how it is off rez. As a wannabe you don't see how it is for full bloods."

"A wannabe?" Conley asked.

"Ya, someone that just visits us for a while, wanting to be Indian, then goes back home," she snapped.

"Oh, I'm sorry you feel that way about me. I don't want to be anything I'm not. I'm just excited about being here and visiting. I want to meet and become friends with some of my grandmother's family, my family. I am glad to be who I am and where I am. I'm proud to be with you and Demi right now," he said in a defensive way from having his feelings hurt.

This was the second time he hadn't felt completely accepted by Terri. She had a way of making Conley keep his ego in check.

They walked up to the hostess desk and were the next in line to be seated. Another couple came in behind them. The hostess took the other couple back to a table. Two more families came in. Soon those families were taken back and seated.

Conley had to say something and tried to be very polite. He just asked the hostess if she had forgot them. The hostess didn't answer and just walked away. Conley was starting to understand.

"Do you run into this kind of treatment often?" Conley asked.

"Ya, often enough," Terri replied. "Now let's go."

"Hold on. I have a plan."

"No! What will happen is this. These people will call the police and then wait until the cops arrive then start a fight and then the cops come in and take us to jail. Now you got the picture?"

"Trust me," Conley said as he saw that there was an empty table out in the middle of the room. He asked the hostess if they could sit there. Again, the hostess didn't say a word and looked away from him. He took Terri's arm and escorted her and Demi to the empty table where he pulled out a chair for Terri, walked over and got a booster seat for Demi and the three of them sat down.

Terri asked, "Do you trust any food they bring us now that you see how they are here? I don't think I want to eat anything. You saw how they looked at us, how rude they were."

"It's okay. I've got this," Conley replied.

After a long wait and everyone else there had already received their food the waitress came to take the order. Conley ordered two steak dinners with baked potatoes and green beans and a fish sandwich for Demi.

The waitress, never saying a word, left with the order and Terri said that Demi doesn't even like fish. Conley just nodded reassurance and smiled. Terri looked very uneasy. After about ten minutes Conley left a nickel on the table and said, "Okay, they have the food cooking by now, let's go and find a place where you want to eat. Maybe Cousin Larry should be called Cousin Buzzard. Cousin Larry can eat our order. And I hope he gets heart burn."

They got up from the table and quickly walked out. Terri laughed all the way to the car. Conley could tell she was definitely in a better mood. Conley thought she seemed relieved that they didn't have to eat the food at a place she didn't trust and had treated them so poorly.

Conley was a bit saddened, some by the stunt he just pulled but mostly by why he did what he did. He thought it was awful how some people treated others. He now had a better understanding of what Terri meant earlier.

They ended up at an ice cream shop where they enjoyed a hamburger and fries and an ice cream sundae for dessert. Conley got a hot fudge sundae and Terri was eating a bowl of peach ice cream while Demi was making the most of a vanilla cone and now she seemed much happier.

They spent the rest of the day together. The first stop was at a small zoo on the edge of town. Conley enjoyed the colorful parrots and for a few minutes had one sitting on his shoulder.

Terri got chills and clung to Conley as they went through the snake house. To Conley's surprise she did love the lizards. The lizards were loose in one section and Terri and Demi had fun looking for them and spotting them as the critters hid among the foliage. This portion of the zoo felt really good because it was sprayed with a cool mist of water over the tropical plants and any of the animals in there running around. Terri even had a rather large lizard in her hand at one point and was petting it.

Conley lead the way into a screened-in room full of butterflies. Inside a lady was taking care of the butterflies and showed them that if they put orange juice on the back of their hand and stood really still a butterfly would land on their hand to eat.

She put a drop of the juice on the back of each of their hands and stood back. Demi went around holding her hand up to the butterflies so they could find her. It was hard to get Demi to stand still but as soon as one landed on Terri's hand Demi stood still because she wanted a butterfly to land on her hand too. It only took a few moments for one of the larger ones to land on Demi's little hand that Conley was helping to hold still. She started to jerk her hand away but Conley held it fast so the butterfly would stay.

Demi looked around to make sure Terri saw her and had a big smile on her sweet face. She didn't seem too sure about it walking around tickling her hand. After the butterfly left her hand she was done with the butterflies and was ready to see what was next.

Demi was watching the turtles swimming in a tank. She would point and Conley saw that her eyes grew big as a turtle would go by close to the glass where she stood.

Outside she got to sit on one of the three giant tortoises while it walked around. At first she was wary about touching one of them. After Terri showed her it was okay to pet them she rubbed its shell. The man there gave Demi some green leaves of some kind to feed them. He said that awhile back they let people sit on them but didn't allow that any longer. He took a look at Demi and said since she was small that she could ride one. He helped her get on top of the tortoises and take a short ride. Demi had big, beautiful, dark brown eyes naturally but her eyes were even bigger now and her face was full of delight.

Next, they drove across town to this playground. Conley had never seen one quite like this one. It had castles and forts. It had play houses that were more like giant doll houses the little girls could walk through and play in. There was even a puppet show off to one side. The park had a maze of sidewalks and was more of a fairytale land than a playground.

Terri put Demi on a merry-go-round and was pushing her slowly. Conley was just looking around at all the unusual things this park offered. Terri ran into a friend from high school and turned away from Demi to talk for a moment when two older boys, not meaning any harm, jumped on the merry-go-round and had it going as fast as they could run in just seconds.

Conley looked around and saw Demi barely holding on. Both her hands were holding the bar but her poor little legs were off the merry-go-round, in fact, her whole body was off the merry-go-round and flying like a flag. Conley jumped and grabbed a push bar next to where Demi was and held on slowing the thing down as fast as he could.

He was right beside Demi when her little arms gave out and she flew off the ride right into Conley's waiting hands. He anticipated her flying off and was ready to catch her or else she would have landed across the lawn over by the duck pond.

Conley could tell it really scared Terri and made her upset that the merry-go-round could even go that fast. It was okay though because Demi thought it was fun. After that thrill ride they walked down and got a cherry slushy which felt good and cooled them down from the heat of the day and the excitement of the joy ride.

Going back to the car they walked past a game booth. The booth was raising money for the animal shelter. The game was filled with small fish bowls and for five dollars you got three ping pong balls to throw at the fish bowls. If you got all three balls in any of the fish bowls you won a giant stuffed animal. There were lesser prizes if you only got one or two ping pong balls in one of the fish bowls.

Terri said, "I never win at those games."

"Me either," Conley said. He remembered his dream but did the dream mean they would win the tiger? What if it meant something else and Demi left disappointed? Conley was half afraid to take that chance.

He kept walking. Demi stopped dead in front of Conley and he almost stepped on her and had to hop to keep his balance and keep from running her over. He looked down and saw Demi standing there with her fingers in her mouth looking back at a large stuffed tiger on the counter. Conley knelt down and asked, "That's a beautiful tiger isn't it?"

Demi nodded with her fingers still in her mouth. Her eyes didn't part from the stuffed toy.

"If you had a tiger like that would you give it a hug?" Conley asked.

"I would crush it," Demi said. She looked at Conley and opened both arms and gave Conley a big hug to show him how she would crush the tiger.

Now Conley was sure.

"Okay, now you can do this. You get three balls and you have to make sure you throw them easy so they will land in the fish bowls. Understand?"

Demi nodded again.

Conley gave the lady five dollars and got the three ping pong balls. He picked Demi up and handed her one of the balls.

She studied for a minute then softly threw the ball. It hit the edge of one fish bowl and bounced into another bowl. Conley handed her another ball. Demi wanted both balls, one in each hand. Conley held her around the waist and leaned forward. Demi moved both hands and let go of the ball in her right hand then tossed the ball in her left hand a second later.

One ball bounced off of several bowls then landed inside one of the fish bowls. The other ball went straight into a bowl. Demi won.

The lady said, "Good job. What animal do you want? How about this cuddly bear?" She pointed to an assortment of different animals to choose from.

Without hesitation Demi ran over and grabbed the tiger and gave it a hug. The tiger was longer than she was tall and she had to use both arms to hold it.

Terri asked, "What do you say?"

Demi looked at the lady and said, "Thank you." She looked at Conley and said, "Thank you. Mommy, look, a tiger. Grrrrrr."

Demi held the tiger tight as they walked on. She wouldn't let anyone help her. It took both of her hands to carry the big toy and even at that the tiger's tail dragged the ground as they walked.

Conley thought a lot of the time his dreams were a curse. He was glad he remembered his dream this time. Seeing the look on Demi's face made his dreams worthwhile.

Later that evening they ended up at the campgrounds by the lake where Conley first camped. After they checked in and put up the tent they walked down to the lake and rented a paddle boat. It was very relaxing as they paddled around an island and watched as people fished and threw bread to the assortment of wild ducks.

Demi was pointing to some trout swimming below the boat. They were in the grass that grew in parts of the lake. Conley told her that they would go fishing and maybe catch one of those trout for dinner later on. Conley could tell by the smile on her face that Demi would like to catch a fish.

After the paddle boat ride they went to the miniature golf course. It only had nine holes to play. Demi had never played miniature golf but once shown how to softly hit the golf ball she had a good time. At first she couldn't hit the ball then she wanted to knock it clear across the lake. All in all she did pretty well.

Next, Conley went and got his fishing pole and some bread. Terri and Demi were using the rest of the bread to throw at the ducks. Conley made a small dough ball out of one piece and helped Demi fish. She did have one strike and was excited as she reeled it in. It was a very small one but she got to touch it and wanted it to go back home to its mommy so Conley set it in the water and they watched as it swam away.

At dark they built a small fire and shortly after that Demi fell asleep in Conley's lap. Terri spoke, "I'm sorry you didn't get to talk with Rose and find out if she was related to you."

"Ah, but I did. Not in person. Last night she came to me by dream and showed me she was my grandmother's sister. I don't have proof but at least I know. And since she was your grandmother's cousin then we are distant cousins from way back down the line somewhere," Conley said telling only part of the dream. Then he asked, "Will you spend a few days with me here? There is still a lot I want to do and see and I would really love for you and Demi to share it with me."

"Ya, Demi would like that. Demi had a great time today."

"And you? Would you like it too?" Conley asked.

Terri grinned and looked down and replied, "Ya, I would like it too. Geez."

# CHAPTER 21

*It is very dark. Someone has a small light but the light doesn't help much. It is very quiet. The only sound is water dripping. The dank smell of moldy dirt is in the air. Conley sits trying to see, trying to listen. There is a movement at the other end of the darkness, or is it just shadows playing tricks? He moves to the far side to investigate. Something jumps out of sight behind a rock in the corner. There is a sound when it jumps. It sounds like bracelet charms or the sound of a very small bell.*

*Conley goes over to where he heard the jingle sound. Nothing is there. He is feeling around and finds a hole in the wall. He hears the hiss of a young cat. He kneels down and looks in the hole to see what he can. A bright light hits his eyes, blinding him for a second. He jumps back and almost falls.*

As he woke he had to put his hand in front of his face to block the sunlight so he could see what was going on. It was Terri. She had opened the tent flap and was crawling into the tent carrying a little kitten she had found wandering around the camp area. She was going to show it to Demi.

"Get up all you sleepy heads," Terri said in a most pleasing good morning sort of way.

Demi stirred and when she saw the little yellow tiger striped kitten her eyes popped wide open as she sat up to see if it was really true. "Mommy, a kitty," she said.

Conley rubbed the kitten's head then headed to the showers to freshen up and get ready for the new day ahead. After his shower he stepped back outside in clean clothes and he could smell the bacon frying.

Conley found Terri at the grill. "You were up early this morning."

Terri nodded. "Yeah, I was awake before anyone else so I walked down to the market." She nodded toward the picnic table. "Bacon, eggs, and milk for Demi." Terri then used a fork to flip a slice of bacon.

Demi was throwing a stick. Then when the kitten didn't go fetch it she would run and get the stick to show the kitten what to do and how to play this game. She would then throw the stick again to see if the kitten learned anything yet.

While they ate Conley watched as Demi tried to force feed her scrambled eggs to the cat and saw the cat was more interested in reaching for her bacon. Conley spoke, "What do we want to do today?"

Terri announced, "I picked up a small bag of apples over at the market and thought we could drive out to Custer State Park where we can watch the herd of buffalo and maybe find the herd of wild donkeys. We can pet them and feed them the apples."

"Sounds like a good plan to me," Conley said.

On the drive over to Custer State Park they took a side trip to the top of one of the rolling hills or foot hills. They drove around and found a very pretty horseshoe shaped waterfall in a stream. They hiked around, admiring the view.

Conley showed Demi how to skip rocks and she would pick some up and put them in her pockets instead of throwing them. Terri said she always had a pocket full of rocks by the end of each day.

At the very top peak of one of the hills they found a spring. There was enough water bubbled out of this spring to form two rather large running creeks. Since the spring was at the very peak half the water ran down one side of the hill and half the water ran down the other side of the hill forming two separate streams. Conley followed the two streams with his eyes for as far as he could see them. He had never seen a spring that formed two creeks like this one did.

He went over and tried to get Demi to throw some rocks into the water and make a splash. She did throw a few but then any of the colorful rocks went into her pockets again.

They drove all over the park looking for the buffalo herd. At one grassy field they saw several antelope about the same size or just a bit smaller than a deer. They were all walking together and grazing in the rich country meadow.

Conley had never seen any antelope and was fascinated with how the horns came out above their eyes and formed a horn that was flat and thicker near the head and went to a point curling inward. The antelope were brown with a white belly and rear end and a blotch of white on its neck with a white face. Terri told him that some of the locals called them pronghorns.

As he was driving something about the size of a small dog ran right out in front of the car. He hit the brakes to avoid running over the poor little guy. "Did you see that poor little shabby lost dog way out here in the wild?" Conley asked.

Terri started laughing hard and it took a few minutes before she could catch her breath and say, "That isn't a dog. It's a porcupine." She thought it was funny that Conley didn't know a dog from a porcupine. The more she thought about it the more tickled she got. Conley could just hear this being told over and over again once they got back to the reservation. He just smiled and they went on.

Conley thought how everyone liked telling a funny story over and over. It reminded him of a scene in the movie *Dances With Wolves* where Kevin Costner had to tell and retell a funny story over and over each time someone new joined them so everyone could laugh. That movie really captured some of the Lakota customs and the ways of the people, especially how they loved and tried to take care of their families.

As they drove through the park they also spotted a couple wild turkeys and some brightly colored pheasant. At one place they slowed down to watch a road runner cross the pavement and run through a bare spot in the field. Conley knew at once that the cartoon had captured the little bird. It ran very fast and its little legs were a blur as it went by. He couldn't resist and had to say, "Beep, beep," as it ran past.

Conley pulled over and got out. There was a majestic looking elk on a hill across the way. He had never seen one of those either. It was almost as big as a cow. It was light brown with a darker brown mane or bushy area around its neck. He just looked at the huge rack of antlers it was carrying. The antlers seemed half the size of its body. He could understand how people would photograph them and even paint them on canvas but he couldn't understand hunting them and killing them.

About a half an hour later they ran across the wild donkeys. They pulled off the road and got out. Terri got the bag of apples and started cutting them in quarters. She said, "Now these animals may seem tame but they're still wild. You can pet them and feed them these apples but they will bite and kick so be careful around them. One of us will have to hold Demi so she won't get stepped on or hurt."

"I've heard of wild horses but never heard of wild donkeys," Conley replied.

"We have wild horses around here too but they don't usually come over to you. These donkeys were left by miners back a hundred years ago. Many found their way to this grassy area and formed a herd and have lived here ever since."

The donkeys wandered over to where they smelled the apples. Maybe they came over from learning that when people came they brought these tasty treats. They were gentle enough. Conley picked Demi up and put a piece of apple in his other hand. One of the donkeys walked up and took the apple and started munching it. He held Demi over to where she could pet the animal. She was just a bit afraid at first because of their size compared to hers but once she touched it then she wanted to feed it an apple too.

Conley told her they both could hold the apple and he helped her give one to the donkey so she would not get her fingers in its mouth. The donkey would use its lips to maneuver the apple slice out of their hand and into its mouth.

They walked around petting many of the cute looking animals. Some of the donkeys were mostly gray or dirty white while others had a darker charcoal color and some were even a reddish color. They all had the dark line down the center of the back and dark lines across the shoulders forming the cross mark donkeys were known for. Most of them had whiter bellies but all of them had a white nose, or muzzle, and long ears.

Another car pulled off the road and parked. A family got out and two of the older boys tried to get on the back of one of the donkeys. That was a mistake. The donkey started bucking and kicking. It took its teeth and bit the leg of the boy and pulled him off very quickly. He was lucky to not have been hurt other than the bruised mark that was left on his leg.

The father yelled at the boys to stop messing around like that. Terri told them to stop because those were wild donkeys and they could hurt people. She was angry because they upset Demi who now didn't want to go close to the donkeys any longer and clung to Conley.

After a bit of trying Conley did get Demi to pet another donkey but the fun was out of it for her. She took the apple piece and ate it herself. Why should the donkeys get all the food? They left and went on to find the buffalo herd.

They were almost out of the park when they finally spotted the large animals, maybe forty or fifty of them, over by some trees. Conley wanted to know if they could feed these animals some apples. "No, and don't get out of the car. These creatures are temperamental. Sometimes you could pet them and they wouldn't mind but then other times they would rather charge you and gore you with those horns. No one really knows what sets them off," Terri instructed.

"Is there something killing some of those pine trees? See how on one side of almost every tree over there it has a huge dished out section where the tree is almost in half?" Conley asked.

"Nay, the buffalo use the trees to scratch their backs and rub against the tree so much that they wear the tree in two eventually. Each buffalo has its own tree and will fight another buffalo if it moves in to take its scratching post away. They use the same tree until it breaks and falls down. The buffalo then gets very angry because his tree fell and it'll have to find another one," Terri shared.

"I see some buffalo fur beside the road over there. I'm going to get it. I'll be careful and not go where any of these giant animals are. Just going to grab that ball of fur for a souvenir and get right back here," Conley reported.

He got out and ran over and picked the ball of buffalo fur up and put it in his pocket and ran and got back in the car just as one of the buffaloes spotted him and walked over his way. The buffalo walked in front of the car and stopped and looked at everyone. It stayed there if front of the car for over a half an hour just staring at them and not letting them leave or go anywhere else. It was a bit weird but really neat to get to see the buffalo up close for that length of time.

Conley watched and studied how magnificent the buffalo looked standing there. Its head was huge and was so big it would never fit through the car's window. From the wooly fur on the front of the animal he could see why it faced the cold wind where other animals faced away from cold wind. A fact he remembered from watching a nature channel.

The wooly fur around its shoulders was a lighter brown than the smooth fur on the back and sides which was a rich dark brown. Its head was covered in even darker brown, almost a black fluffy fur that covered the shape of its head and hung down in front covering its chest area. Conley could only see its black nose and eyes which looked lost in all that fur. It had two short horns that rose out of the fur just past its eyes pointing up to the top of its head.

Once the buffalo in front of them moved Conley left slowly driving off. They had one more place to visit that day. After driving for a bit they pulled into the entrance to visit the Crazy Horse Memorial. At the gate Conley stopped to pay. Terri told them she was an Oglala and the man let them in for free.

They drove up to the Native American Center to start with and went in. It was an open area inside this big building where Native Americans could set up to sell their crafts. It also allowed for entertainment and today there was a man playing an Indian flute with several people standing around listening. He was quite good and had some CDs and some flutes for sale he had hand made.

After one of his songs a lady asked, "All the songs seem so sad. Could you play something happy?"

He looked at her puzzled and replied, "The song I just played was a wedding song. I don't know any songs any happier than that one."

Conley bought one of his CDs and after looking over most of the flutes on the table the three of them walked over to the main building and went in the restaurant there to order dinner.

Terri and Demi just got chicken fingers to share. Terri added a salad and Demi got mac and cheese. Conley ordered a buffalo steak to see if it was any good. He read on the menu where it had seventy percent less fat, fifty percent less cholesterol and forty percent more protein than beef and wanted to try it.

It was delicious. It was tender and had a mild beef flavor and didn't have any wild game taste like Conley thought it might.

After lunch they went through the museum building. Conley saw some really neat things and learned about how life used to be way back when. He spotted the Indian headdress, or war bonnet as it is sometimes called. He was impressed with all the feathers that were made to look like eagle feathers mounted into the headdress.

Where each feather was mounted to the war bonnet it had little colorful feathers added and at the tip of each eagle like feather was a strand of horse hair extending past the tip and hanging down. There were two thin strips of fur, one on each side, which added to the beauty of the bonnet. It had a beaded band that ran along the front at the forehead. The feathers fanned out and reminded him of all the cowboy movies he used to watch as a kid with his dad.

The one he liked the best was called a roach. It was a narrow headdress that went down the center of the head. It only had two feathers standing straight up coming out from the top and the rest of the roach was made from hair of some sort.

Terri told him she used to help her grandfather make them when she was younger. She said the hair was from the tail of a deer. The hair was sewn in just a few at a time along the entire edge and this was how the hair stood up instead of falling over. This type headdress was for men only and it was used more in battle than the other type headdresses. They were dyed to a color that meant something to the warrior or the tribe.

Conley wanted to go through the gift shop so Terri said she and Demi would be outside. The shop had lots of paintings. Conley learned that the Red Cloud School in Pine Ridge taught art and that many Native Americans learned how to express themselves drawing and painting. By selling the art work many young people earned money to add to their livelihoods.

He looked around and saw a painting of a warrior on a horse running in a snow storm. The artist was his friend, Longknife. He liked the painting and since he had met and talked with Longknife he bought it and had it sent back to his tin can castle.

When Conley walked back outside he looked around and found Terri and Demi standing down at the end of the overlook deck that faced the mountain being carved into a statue of Chief Crazy Horse sitting on his mount. They had been working on this project for over fifty years and it was just now shaping up so one could see what it was going to look like. When finished, this will be the largest granite carving in the world.

Conley remembered seeing an article about this when he was in the fourth grade. The article was in the Weekly Reader newspaper they got at school every so often.

What a picture in his mind; Terri and Demi standing there with this giant stone horse just beyond them on the mountain across the way.

Seeing Terri and the giant stone horse behind her woke a memory of a dream.

Conley started to go toward Terri when he saw a man hiding behind a potted tree. Before he could get to the man, the guy jumped out and grabbed Terri from behind and swung her around by her waist. Demi gave out a squeal.

Conley ran over and pushed the man away from Terri and seeing the scar on his face was ready to fight him. The man looked surprised and just stood there. Terri shouted, "What are you doing? This is my friend from high school."

"Oh, so you're alright?" Conley asked.

"Yeah, I'm alright. What's the matter with you?" Terri asked half angry at Conley's actions.

Conley relaxed and said, "I'm very sorry. I thought you were hurting Terri. Again I'm so sorry. My name is Conley." He then extended his hand in greeting to meet Terri's friend.

Terri then said, "This is Joseph and I have known him most of my life."

"I guess you scared me a little when I saw you swinging Terri around and heard Demi yell," Conley said. This time his dream got him in a little hot water and he felt bad about it. He felt very awkward from misunderstanding his dream. The dream had shown him what had happened but he mistook the meaning of it and was glad no one was in trouble. He knew he had dreamed of Joseph for some reason though and wanted to stay close just in case there was something more going to happen, maybe something he dreamed of and forgot.

"No problem. Hey, I'm going over to check out this mine I found. Wanna come with me?" Joseph asked looking at Terri.

"Sure," Terri answered. She looked at Conley and said, "I know Dad has you looking after me but I'm a big girl and I take care of myself. I'll ride with Joseph if that is okay with you."

"Yes, are you sure you even want me to come along? I didn't mean any harm. I would like to go but if you rather I didn't I would understand," Conley replied.

"Yes, you can come. I want to ride with Joseph so we can talk. I haven't seen him for a while is all," Terri said.

"Okay, I'll follow then," Conley said as they headed for their cars.

# CHAPTER 22

The old red pickup truck Conley was following pulled up an incline just off one of the back roads onto a short gravel area off the roadway. There was only room for two or three cars. Conley looked around as he turned off his car. He could see up ahead a path that lead up toward a cliff.

Conley and the others followed the rutted out path up toward the cliff to where he could see an opening that went inside the mountain. Conley noticed everyone was looking at the gravel and other small rocks along the path to see if they could spot gold even before they got to the mine.

Joseph picked up one small rock that looked like gold but upon further examination Joseph told everyone that what he found was pyrite crystals or fool's gold as he showed it to the others. He did say that gold would look quite a bit like the rock he found and that is why it was called fool's gold and the pyrite crystals fooled many miners through the years.

The path was overgrown with weeds and wild flowers and it looked as if it had been a long time since anyone had been here. They all stood in front of this opening while Joseph checked his flashlight.

There was a gigantic granite boulder six feet above a small opening. The opening had very old wood timbers on both sides forming a door and a long timber across the top acting as a brace to hold the boulder above it from falling in. Conley noticed that one side of the timber forming the door was bowed and had been dished out much like the trees the buffalos used to scratch their backs.

He saw where long ago in the dried out wood two sets of initials were carved deeply into the face of the timber. One was JJ and the other was FJ so maybe Jesse James and his brother Frank had been in this area after all.

Conley and the others peered into the doorway with the flashlight to check and see if they could make anything out on the inside before going in. Joseph had to hit the flashlight a few times on the palm of his hand then the light came on brighter. The mine wasn't very far into the mountain and they could see the back wall about forty or fifty yards ahead.

Conley followed Terri and Joseph through the doorway and stood inside the mine. Conley was holding Demi's hand and she was squeezing his hand tight. They had to stop for a few minutes to allow their eyes to adjust to the darkness.

The tunnel leading to the back was about eight feet wide and it was about six or seven feet high so there was plenty of room to walk. It led to the back where it opened up into a rather large room maybe half the size of a basketball court.

At first the flashlight didn't seem very bright but as Conley's eyes adjusted the hand held light gave off enough light to see most of what was inside.

Conley and the others walked to the end of the mine looking for any shiny gold colored rocks and to see what the miners from days past had left. The mine was empty except for an old rusty pick without a handle lying over to one side.

Conley watched as Terri and Joseph checked the walls for any sign of gold or silver and the floor of the cave for the same. There was one section that was dug out forming a small corridor off to the left. Terri was looking at a vein of light brown colored rock running through the middle of the wall in this corridor.

From the light Conley could see sparkles from some sort of mica that went through out the vein. Terri pointed to a few small quartz crystals in the vein. Joseph was using the pick head to chip away at the vein to see if there was anything of interest.

Demi was turning over some rocks on the ground to see what was under them. She really got into hunting for gold. Conley smiled at her for working so hard and being so seriously.

Terri was ahead of the rest of the group when she gave out a scream. Conley jumped. She came back to the others in a hurry. She pointed over to the corner where she just vacated and said, "There's a skeleton over there. Something big died."

Conley and Joseph walked slowly over to where Terri just came from and looked. There was a large skeleton. Conley was relieved to see that it wasn't a skeleton of a human. It looked to be the bones of a donkey.

There was an old, mostly rotten, rope still tied around its neck going over and around a large rock. Someone had left it there and just let it die. Demi wanted to see but Terri grabbed her away and told her not to go over there. She took Demi over to the back side of the mine to look for gold there to keep her away from seeing the bones of the donkey.

Joseph trying to be funny and turned the light off and gave out a blood curdling scream just to scare everyone. He did a great job too. Conley jumped and heard Terri and Demi give out a scream at the same time. Joseph turned the light back on, laughing. He was so loud that Conley almost didn't notice the low rumbling sound. A deep drone of sound and movement that Conley felt in his feet first.

Conley stopped laughing. The noise grew louder, more threatening. Terri squealed, and they started for the entrance.

It was too late.

There was a crash of timbers and a big boom. More cracking as wood broke in the tunnel near the opening. The timbers split apart as a gigantic rock from above the doorway shifted. It crashed down over the opening they had just came through moments before. The light from outside disappeared. The cave went dark.

Terri and Demi screamed. Conley's heart sped up, and he felt a prickle of uneasy sweat down his neck. He was breathing hard. They all stood still for some seconds.

"What the heck just happened?" Joseph asked.

Conley checked to make sure no one was hurt. Conley tried to make sure everyone was okay and reassure them the best he could that they would all be okay but their faces had a look of panic and fear on them. They waited until no more rumbling sound was heard and the choking dust had cleared then Conley slowly walked over to where the mine caved in to see if he could maybe dig their way out.

He saw that they couldn't move any rocks and clear an opening because it wasn't like a cave in a Hollywood set or what he had seen in movies. This cave in was just the one monstrous boulder that had fallen through the roof and now blocked the entire entrance. There was nothing to dig out.

"Let's look around some more. There has to be something here that can help us," Conley suggested.

The flashlight was getting dimmer and Joseph had to hit the light on his palms every few minutes. Conley knew they would all be in the dark very soon.

"Joseph, take the light back down where the donkey is and look around. We didn't check that area very good," Conley said.

"I'm getting a little bit cold," Terri said.

"Hey, I have a magnifying glass and if we find some wood and sunshine I can build a fire," Joseph said.

Conley couldn't believe what he just heard. "Tell me you were being silly otherwise that was just a crazy statement."

"Yeah, I guess that was a dumb thing to say especially out loud," Joseph said.

Demi, imitating Joseph when he yelled, was now hollering "Hey!" She could hear it echo once every time she did it and that seemed to tickle her. She would yell "Hey" then listen. When she heard the echo, Conley noticed that she looked around to see who else thought that was amazing. No one paid her much attention at her new found art form. Conley could tell Terri and Joseph was getting upset with her so Conley walked over to her and gave her a hug.

Conley said, "That's really neat, Demi. You're hearing your own words coming back to you after they bounce off the cave walls. That's called an echo. Do you like that?"

She nodded her head yes and smiled.

Conley thought Demi was probably the bravest. Conley felt this was because she probably hadn't realized the danger they were in and thought it was just dark. Conley could tell she didn't seem to mind and she went around picking up rocks and putting them in a pile and then kicking the rocks toward the back of the mine, yelling "*Boom*" when she kicked.

"Look at this. There are some old saddle bags under the donkey bones. The only thing I found in one of them was this old copper can thing. Probably just junk," Joseph said.

"Let me see what you have there, Joseph," Conley said.

Joseph handed Conley the odd looking treasure he had found. "What in the world is this?" Joseph asked.

Conley examined the newfound item. It was about the size of half a can of food and had a copper tube coming out of the top into a little valve that was mounted on the back side of a copper funnel shaped disk.

"If this is what I think it is you did real well, Joseph," Conley said.

The flashlight grew very dim and then flickered and went dead. Joseph tried and tried hitting it on his palm to make it come back on but the batteries were too far gone.

"Now what do we do?" Terri asked in the pitch black darkness.

Demi was whimpering now.

"We may be okay here in a minute. Terri just hold Demi close so she won't get too frightened. Give me a minute to finish checking out this thing Joseph found," Conley said in a calm voice.

Conley tried to turn the top of the canister like he was opening a jar. He picked up a rock and was tapping the edge of the can to break it loose. After much grunting and letting a few cuss words slip out, the seal broke. Conley unscrewed the top and put his finger down into the canister. He felt a fine power and more chunks of something inside the can. He used a long thin stone to dig some of the chunks loose and tried to break them into small pieces as best he could.

"Now we need to find some water. I don't mean like a whole glass full, just enough to put some inside this can here," Conley said.

Terri started moving. "I slipped in some mud over by the far wall." She and Demi crawled on the ground and found the wet spot. "Here it is."

"Good. Now find where water is dripping and then dish out a spot in the dirt to hold some of the water. I need some for this lantern Joseph found," Conley said.

"That was a lantern?" Joseph asked.

"Yes it is. I just hope we can get it to work. My grandfather had one of these and I used to play with it when I was a small kid. It's called a carbide miner's lamp and was used by coal miners a long time ago. I guess it was also used by gold miners, or so it seems."

They had to wait for the water to fill the small handmade pond Terri had dug out with her fingers. The water dripping from the roof of the cave only dripped a few drops of water every other couple of minutes. It took what seemed like a long time before they could hear the water starting to make a splashing sound when it dripped.

They were all sitting next to the miniature pool just waiting in the dark. Demi was clinging to Terri and her whimpers were getting louder and coming more often.

"It's going to be okay, baby doll. I hope to get us some light goin' in just a few more minutes," Conley said.

"What if it doesn't work?" Joseph asked.

"Well, let's not think like that. There's always something else we can figure out if we have to. Maybe a torch of some sort. For now this lantern is the answer. We just need to get some water in with the carbide so it will make gas," Conley said.

"It's not going to blow us up is it?" Terri asked.

"No way. It's not that powerful," Conley replied.

Conley waited until he couldn't wait any longer. He took off one of his socks and soaked it in the water so not to get any mud into the container. When the sock was soaked enough he held it over the can and squeezed the sock allowing the water to fall into the canister. He listened. He repeated this action until the water on the cave floor was all used up. He listened again. This time he heard a fizzing sound as the water interacted with the carbide.

"I hope this works," he said and then screwed the top back on the canister. "Terri, I need your lighter."

"Umm, I left it in the truck," she replied.

"Okay, Joseph, crawl around until you find the old pick and bring it to me," Conley said.

After a few minutes of Joseph stumbling around in the dark he said, "Here it is. I found it."

He crawled back over to Conley and handed the pick head to him. The gas formed from the water and carbide was still hissing so Conley held the lantern next to a large rock he was hoping was granite. He took the pick head and started chipping the rock while holding the lantern next to where he was chipping away with the pick. Finally there was a spark.

*Whoosh.* The lantern fired up with a flurry from all the gas that had been escaping. There was a smell of burning hair when the flame singed the hair around Conley's hand where he was holding the lantern. The flame settled down and was burning with a steady flame. It didn't give off as much light as a fully charged flashlight but it was better light than they had towards the end just before Joseph's flashlight died out.

Demi went back to work and again she gathered up another small pile of tiny rocks and kicked them yelling "Boom" and then she would listen for her echo and smile. This time when she did this Conley thought he saw something move toward the back of the cave or was it a shadow playing tricks on him?

He was looking at the back wall when he saw something move again. This time he thought he heard something. "Shh, listen," he said. "Did you hear that? Bells. I thought I heard a tiny sleigh bell, no, a smaller jingle sound."

"I don't hear anything," Joseph said.

The only sound was a dripping sound of some water falling a few drips at a time from the roof of the cave. Demi kicked her rock pile again with another boom yell and this time Conley saw something jump over a stone and was disappearing like the Cheshire Cat. This time they all heard the jingle sound of a tiny bell from somewhere in the back of the mine.

Conley hurried to the back and was checking around to see what he could find. He felt around the rock where he saw something jump and vanish. There was a small opening and he knelt down on one knee. He held the lantern close and peered into the small hole that was near the bottom of the wall on the floor of the mine. He saw two small eyes of green light looking back at him. He jumped back and almost fell over some rocks behind him.

There was a small sound that was half growl or squall and half grunt that a cat makes without even opening its mouth then a hiss and the little cat ran on back through the hole and was gone.

"This may be a way out. It looks like maybe it is an old ground hog or badger tunnel. The bell was on a cat and he went through here. I think with some effort we can dig out of this dark dingy place," Conley said.

Joseph grabbed the old pick head and handed it to Conley. The earth was soft here and the hole was almost big enough to crawl through so he thought it wouldn't take them very long to dig to the outside.

Conley and Joseph took turns digging. They dug along the same path the cat followed making it bigger and wider. They had to dig out the top and sides big enough for a person to crawl through and rake the dirt back into the cave. It was hard to move in such a small tunnel. They had to dig then back out of the small hole to pull the dirt away and back into the mine so they could wiggle back in the hole and dig some more. The longer they made the opening the longer it took to move the dirt out of the tunnel and back into the mine to give them room to dig some more but they were making progress.

As Conley and Joseph dug they had to follow the opening as it turned and went around bends which made the digging harder. They thought about digging straight but wasn't sure if straight would lead them to the outside so following the tunnel was the only option.

When they stopped to catch their breath Demi would crawl to the hole and look in to see if she could see anything. Conley thought it was cute how she would use her hands and feet to crawl without letting her knees touch the cold damp dirt. Once when Conley crawled out from digging Demi went over to him and was helping by brushing some of the dirt off Conley's jeans using her hands. She was such a good helper.

After going in about eleven or twelve feet they could hear some water running ahead and could hear something that sounded like leaves blowing in the wind. They could feel fresh air and a small puff of wind once in a while. There was just a speck of light ahead too.

While Joseph was taking his turn digging Conley sat down to rest. He had pulled his knees up to his chest and was hugging them with his arms. He looked over and there sat Demi with her knees up to her chest and she had her arms around her knees imitating Conley. Conley smiled at her then she started rocking back and forth.

Conley wasn't used to needing help. Today he was thinking how grateful he was to have Joseph helping. He was trying to be a better person and wanted others to know how he felt. He crawled over to the opening and squatted down.

"Joseph, can you hear me?" he asked.

"Ya," a muffled voice from inside the small tunnel said.

"Just wanted to say thanks for all the help. You're doing a great job and I appreciate it," Conley said.

"Ya, okay, no problem," Joseph said.

Conley was trying to be a new man ever since his vision quest. He found that the new behavior wasn't so hard for him to do. The hard part was the remembering to do them. He was starting to realize that life was a lot like his dreams. There were parts of life that he had to put together just like his dream puzzle pieces.

Conley was starting to see that he was so involved with figuring out his dreams that he was letting some of his life pass by and he was missing parts of it. From now on he hoped to take more of his real awake life in and be a part of it instead of just watching it looking for clues from his dreams. He had always shown up for his life but now wanted to be a participant in what was going on around him. It would take a little work but he accepted the challenge.

After another hour and a half of digging Conley could see outside and see trees and even a small creek with a little water running down the hill next to where they were. He was never so glad to hear a bird not far away. He finally got his head within about a couple of yards from the outside opening and took a big breath of fresh air. It wouldn't be very long now.

Conley felt a spider web in his face and something was crawling on his head but he couldn't get his hand to his head to knock it off. He could feel the spider web on his face and attached to his eyelids. He had to spit to try and get the web out of his mouth.

Feeling the web jogged Conley's memory. He was thinking of the dream of the two webs. He remembered that one web would harm him and the other would save him and he knew which one this spider web was. He felt very jittery and wanted to get out of the tiny tunnel he was in. He could feel panic setting in. Conley scooted back into the cave as fast as he could.

He knew from the dream that something was about to happen and he didn't like the eerie feel of the web on his face and the spider somewhere on his head. He wanted it off.

"Ouch!" he exclaimed. "The damn thing just bit me."

He scooted back into the mine and stood up. He was brushing his head off as fast as he could. He felt his head burning and he started feeling dizzy. He saw the ground coming up at him fast and then there was no light and no sound even before he fell, face first into the dirt on the cave floor in front of him.

# CHAPTER 23

T he old Indian woman is standing beside the leaning tree and motioning for Conley to come to her. As he walks to her he feels very light and it is almost like he floated to where she is standing.

When he joins her at the tree he is reminded of the blue dream catcher she had made for him. Rose answers before he even asks anything. "You know how the dream catcher works. It collects all dreams and the bad ones are trapped in the webbing and the good ones are allowed to float down the feather back to you. Each of us has different colors we connect with. Your color is blue so that is the color of your gift from me."

She points over toward Dillon Pass and when Conley looks he sees people going into Martin's barn a couple miles away. They are carrying someone in and putting him on a bench. He watches as Little Wolf prays. Little Wolf goes over to the person lying there and is changing the bandage around some wound on his head. He puts some herbs on the wound. He then shakes a rattle and there is sage burning beside this person.

The old Indian woman speaks, "That is you. You will heal but it will take maybe a week or more."

"How is that me?" Conley asks.

"You are dreaming. I have come to you in your dream to talk with you."

"How am I doing that?" he asks.

*"You are not doing it. I can bring dreams to others. You are aware enough to realize what your dreams do for you. You have learned how to see what is going to happen through your dreams but you are not advanced enough to bring dreams to others yet. You may never find how to make this happen. I will stay with you and guide you sometimes. I will help you understand and protect you."*

*"Haven't you crossed over?" Conley asks.*

*"Yes, but that doesn't mean I no longer exist." Conley sees a smile on Rose's face.*

*"But you look so real," Conley says.*

*"I am real, very real. You don't think dreams are real? I know you know better than that after all the dreams you have had.*

*"Actually I am much freer now. So as you use your dreams to help others always remember your vision quest. What you learned there will help keep you safe and on the right path. Dreaming can be used for good or for selfish purposes. Your vision will remind you to use dreams for only good," she answers.*

*"I will always remember my vision quest," Conley says.*

*She watches Conley for a moment then continues, "It is easier to help those you have a kinship with and that is another reason you have to understand that we are all related. Also know that a dream is just as real to the unconscious mind as what we call reality is to being awake so what I am saying to you today is as real as if we were together before I crossed over."*

*She points east and when Conley looks east he sees his home. He sees Emily picking up his mail and going inside to make sure everything is as it should be while he is away. Emily looks as if she isn't concerned about anything and she has everything under control as she puts his mail on the kitchen table. Then Emily goes over to a bare place on the wall and starts hanging a new picture in the dining area. She is just being a good friend and being herself.*

*"Why are you showing me my tin can castle, I mean my home?"*

*"I need to know if you want to stay here or go back home and return here another time."*

*"I guess I will go home for now. I would love to come back again very soon though," he answers.*

"I asked while you are dreaming because usually in a dream we speak from the heart. It is easier while dreaming to know what the heart needs," she says.

"How will I get back home in the condition I'm in over at Martin's barn?"

"You need not worry about that. This Emily I just saw in your dream a second ago, is she the one you want Terri to call?" she asks.

"Yes, Emily will know what to do. How will Terri know to call Emily?"

The old Indian woman smiles and says, "Terri will dream what she should in order to help you. She will dream to call Emily. She will dream to check your phone and find Emily's number, though she may not even remember dreaming. I have told you I can bring dreams to others if it is what is needed in order to help."

Rose chuckles and Conley sees a smile on her face. "Most people get ideas and remember things because of dreams and don't even remember dreaming. They believe they are the ones that think of things when it is their guide reminding them or showing them things through dreams they don't know they just had."

"Is that why some people say they have to sleep on it before making a major decision?" Conley asks.

"You are correct. They know if they sleep on it they get a better answer most of the time and don't realize why," Rose says.

Conley understood this and he asks, "May I cross over with you just to see what it is like? Not to stay, but just look. Is it possible for me to just take a peek?"

She smiles and says, "I am afraid not. If you were to try and cross over the bridge between the two worlds now the bridge would break. You are too heavy. You are still Earth bound.

"It's as beautiful as you have probably read in stories. It is like a newborn coming into this world and seeing everything for the first time. There is no pain or worry. It is an understanding that everything is good. It's as if you are embraced with all the love you can handle at one time."

"Did you turn into an angel when you crossed over?" Coney asks.

*"Nay, I am not an angel. I am just the woman in your dreams."*
Conley sees a sparkle shine from her at her own play on words.
*"Are you a ghost?"* he asks.

*"Nay, I'm not a ghost. A ghost is a lost spirit that can't find the
bridge to cross over to the other side. A ghost's energy is still roaming
the Earth and is stuck there. Sometimes people can see or get a glimpse
of a ghost when they are awake.*

*"My energy has found and returned to its center. I am in spirit
form now. I can only come to you when you dream. My connection to
everything is found in my center and not from the outside.*

*"Once you cross over then the physical world is more dreamlike
than when you lived here. The spirit world is more real. Earth is
made of illusions and shadows while the other side is bright and full
of truth. Life on Earth is always changing just like dreams change,"*
Rose says.

*"How do the dreams work? I mean, how is it possible to dream
of things to come?"*

*"Seeing things to come happens when there is no fear and the
mind is calm. That's why it is easier to do when you are dreaming,"*
Rose says.

Conley asks another question, *"What else can dreams do?"*

*"From dreams you can find items lost. You can get answers to
questions. You get a glimpse of things to be. All of these you already
know. You can also visit places as you have just learned. You can talk
to people that have crossed over as you are doing now. You can send
others dreams or see into their dreams as you may learn some day. You
can share dreams with others as you may learn. You can communicate
through dreams as you are experiencing now. In your dreams you can
go ahead in time or back in time as you are already doing without
thinking about it. There is so much more dreams can do, more than
you are ready to even understand now. For instance dreams can be
used to heal people as Black Elk did and you will even learn to dream
while you are awake."*

*"Dream while I am awake?"* Conley asks.

*"Yes, you did this once already on your vision quest. You've
just scratched the surface. You've just barely started on your dream*

*adventures. Only few even have the ability you already have. I am a dreamwalker. I'm your dream guide. I will help you learn how to use your dreams. And because you are aware, I will guide you but not when you want me to but rather when you need me to," Rose says.*

*"Is that the same as daydreaming?" Conley asks.*

*"It's something like daydreaming. They are very similar except daydreaming is more of consciences attempts of letting the mind roam free.*

*"You have twin daughters that are just now starting to dream the same way you do. I will guide you so later in their life you can guide them," Rose says.*

*"Thank you. This is the very reason I made this trip out here to find you. Did I understand the one dream correct and that you are my grandmother Violet's sister?" he asks.*

*"You are correct. She is my sister."*

*"Can you show me where she is?" he asks.*

*"Nay, your grandmother would have come to you to guide your dreams but she has a different purpose. She has dreams that will save hundreds maybe thousands of soldiers in a war overseas and many of those men and women are Native Americans."*

*"I thought you could dream and find her," Conley says.*

*"I can."*

*"I don't understand," Conley asks out of confusion.*

*Rose says, "There are laws that govern dreams. I cannot ride my pony into someone else's field without being invited to be there."*

*"But you came to me," Conley says.*

*"Yes, you asked for help when you were a child. I had to wait until you were ready to receive my help," Rose answers.*

*"But you are going to send a dream to Terri that will help me," Conley says trying to figure out the situation.*

*"Yes, she has wished there was something she could do to help. So always be careful what you wish for."*

*He can tell his dream is just starting to fade. He wants to ask more, so much more but the dream is almost gone. He wants to understand how to do all this by dreaming. He hopes he didn't ask too late. "When will I learn all this?" he asks one last question.*

*In the distance he hears one last soft statement before his dream is over, "You will learn when it is time."*

*Conley can feel a soft vibration and hear a faint hum. He feels at peace. He feels like he is floating in the heavens. His mind is floating like a cloud until it dissolved into the nothingness, into the consciences of his mind's sky where it could no longer feel or be seen.*

# CHAPTER 24

C onley felt a noodle in his mouth so he swallowed. He searched his mind for Rose but she was gone. There was another noodle in his mouth and he swallowed again. Someone chatted far away. Something came toward his face again, and then there was a spoon in his mouth with another noodle. He swallowed again, mechanically.

Conley felt like he was just waking up. He blinked. His eyes were already open. He tried to focus. A table sat in front of him, very much like his dining table at home, scarred, and a little beat-up.

He focused to see who was there. A picture on the far wall showed a horse being ridden by a brave in a snow storm. He remembered seeing that picture but not on his own wall. He shook his head; he was getting a little confused.

Conley wondered if he was dreaming.

Here came the spoon with another noodle on it. He swallowed. Who was doing this to him? He didn't see anyone. He listened. He could now hear some of the chatting. It was closer now. It sounded like Emily talking to him without giving him time to answer or say anything.

He could see the spoon with a noodle coming toward his mouth once more. This time he bit down on the spoon and the spoon stayed in his mouth. He heard someone say "Opps, sorry about that," and try to remove the spoon. He bit down again and it was harder to get the spoon out of his mouth. The voice stopped. There was a face in front of his. It looked like Emily. The face called his name, "Conley?"

Next he started understanding some of the words that were being said. Then he could hear her say that she was going to give up her apartment and move close to him so she could take care of him. Why did she say that?

He blinked again. He focused on the face. It was Emily. What was she doing here? He didn't remember her coming out to South Dakota. Coming out to where? Where was he?

He stood up. Emily asked, "Conley, do you have to go to the bathroom again?"

He looked down. Emily had both his hands and was leading him across the room. He stopped. She pulled on his arms. He pulled back. He didn't want to go to the bathroom. Emily stopped and took her hands to his face and turned his head so he could look at her. She looked into his eyes. "Conley?" she asked again sounding very concerned.

Conley opened his mouth to say something but nothing came out. He tried again. This time he just made a sound that sounded to him like a crow. He swallowed. He tried to talk again. "Co, co, co, coffee." He struggled but finally got the word out.

Now Emily had her hands up to her face. "Conley! You're back. Welcome home," she exclaimed. She took Conley back over to the table and sat him back down. She then poured him a cup of coffee from the pot she had fixed earlier for herself.

Okay, he was home. Emily was here. But what had happened? How did he get here? Was his trip out west just one of his dreams? His mind was working faster than his body right now and he didn't care for that much.

He looked down at the cup of coffee on the table. He raised his hand to take the cup but his hand only made it to the table then it just sat there beside his coffee. Emily picked up the cup and held it to his lips and let him take a sip.

She let out a small little laugh. "Yep, you are back. How do you feel? Can you understand what I am saying yet?"

Why was she talking to him like he was a dumb ole dodo bird of some kind? More than that, why was he feeling like a zombie? No wonder she was talking to him this way.

His hand made it to the cup this time and he let out a quick startled noise. His hand felt hot. Emily removed his hand from the hot cup. He had bumped the cup and spilled some of the coffee on his hand. Emily held the cup again to his lips so he could take another sip.

He moved his head to look over at her. She had a tear running down her face. He lifted his hand to her face and with the back of his hand he wiped the tear away. That made many more tears fall. Why was she crying?

She leaned forward and gave him a long and tight hug. He made his hand move over to the roll of paper towels on the table and tried to get one. She laughed and then he could hear her sniff a few times as she helped him get a paper towel and she put it in his hand. He took the paper towel and handed it to her and she laughed again even as more tears fell.

He looked around the room and said, "I'm home," halfway making a statement and halfway asking.

"You have been home over a week," Emily told him.

"Are my daughters okay?" he asked.

"Yes, they stopped over yesterday and will be back later today to see you. They will be glad to see you are better and will want to hear all about your trip," Emily said.

"Did I go on a trip?" he asked. His mind was still foggy and he was trying to put things together.

"Yes, you were gone several weeks," Emily replied. "Don't you remember?"

Conley thought a few minutes. His trip to the reservation must not have been a dream after all. "Did I go out west? Did I meet Indians?" he paused then said, "Coffee."

Emily gave him another drink. "Yes, you did. You got hurt and then you got sick and had to come home but you're going to be okay now," Emily told him.

Conley was remembering bits and pieces and some of it was coming together for him and starting to make sense.

He pointed to the picture on the wall of the horse being ridden in the snow and said, "Longknife painted that. I met him."

He thought for a minute and then realized what Emily had said. He remembered getting hurt, but sick? "How'd I get sick?" he asked.

"I was told it was a spider bite. The spider was poisonous and it bit you in your head wound. The poison went into your brain. After that you blacked out and they knew, somehow, to call me and then they sent you home. I talked to a guy named John. He said you stayed some with him."

"Yes, Chief He-Dog." Conley then let out a small laugh.

"He was a chief?" Emily asked.

"Not really. He just told me that so I would buy some . . ." he paused. "Where's my stuff from my trip?"

"It's over by the couch. I haven't unpacked any of it yet," Emily said.

Conley got up and slowly staggered over to where his bag was on the floor beside the couch. Emily walked beside him, holding his waist, making sure he could make it alright without falling. He sat in the floor and opened his bag and searched around until he spotted something rolled up in tissue paper. He unwrapped the paper and took the pair of earrings and handed them to Emily. "Here, I bought these for you. John made them."

He hoped Emily would at least like them. He knew her view points on things like this and knew these earrings wouldn't be her favorite thing to wear. He did hope she at least liked them some. He figured she would at least wear them once to make sure he saw her with them on.

From the many talks they had about the differences between western and country he knew she was all country. She had let him know that western was different than country and some people could mix the two and for some people it worked. He figured there was probably even a difference between western and Native

American if you got right down to it. He thought a little Native American could be mixed with western if one wanted to.

Conley saw something else in his bag. He pulled out the ten inch hunting knife with the bone handle. It had a note with it. He held the note for a minute then opened and read it. "I was unsure if I should send this knife to you or keep it. Demi saw the knife and pointed to it and said 'Conley' and I had no idea why but I knew then it belonged to you. See you later. Your cuz, Little Wolf."

"I remember now. We were trapped in a gold mine. We were crawling to get out when something bit me and that is the last thing I knew until just now. Do you know if Demi and Terri are okay?" Conley asked.

"Yes, they're okay. She's the one that called me. She said you saved them and found the way out. She said they took you to Little Wolf and he did a healing of some sort using some herbs he put on your wound and burned sage and shook a rattle over you all night as he prayed.

"She said Demi had both of her pants pockets full of gold nuggets when they got home. Then she put her dad, John, on the phone to find out what to do with you. So we decided it was best to put you on a plane and get you back here. I've called them every day since to give them a report on your condition. You'll have to call them later today with some good news for a change," Emily said as she sat in the floor next to where Conley was sitting. Sitting slightly behind him she had one of her arms around his shoulder and the other hand patting his leg.

Conley pulled one more item out of his duffle bag. It was the blue dream catcher. Emily gently touched the eagle feather hanging down from the bottom. With the tip of her finger she lightly touched the webbing like she thought she would break it and said, "This is a very pretty dream catcher."

Conley remembered about the dream, the two webs. One web would harm him and one web would save him.

Conley looked at the dream catcher then at Emily. He studied her face as she sat looking in awe of the work put into the catcher. He gave a sly grin then said, "It does two things."

"Two things?" Emily asked. She seemed interested. "I know how it works with dreams but what else does it do?"

Conley held it up in-between him and Emily. He said, "Here let me show you. Put your hand flat on the webbing like this." Conley then put his hand flat on the webbing on one side while Emily carefully put her hand flat against the webbing on the other side. They pressed their hands together with the dream catcher in the middle.

Conley let his finger go through the web and he interlaced his fingers with Emily's fingers. She looked at him puzzled. As they held hands like this Conley looked into Emily's eyes and said, "It also catches the one you love."

Emily's cheeks flushed. A little moisture formed in the corners of her eyes. As if not knowing exactly what to do or say, she said, "Just so you know, coffee and noodles does not count for my 'thank you' dinner."

"Nothing happens unless first we dream," Carl Sandburg.

# About the Author

David C. Dillon attended Miami University. He has two daughters now married with each having a daughter of their own. He lives in southwestern Ohio, in-between Dayton and Cincinnati, in his tin can castle with his cat, Fluffy. He is retired and now loves to write. His hobbies are playing poker, fishing, visiting powwows, and traveling.

For more information visit: www.davidcdillon.us